ROBOTA

ART AND STORY BY
DOUG CHIANG

TEXT BY
ORSON SCOTT CARD

CHRONICLE BOOKS
SAN FRANCISCO

For my wife, Liz, and my sons, Jake and
Ryan, whose love and encouragement have
helped me through the many long nights
and weekends spent completing this book.
To Ralph McQuarrie for his constant inspiration, vision, and friendship.

Library of Congress Cataloging-in-
Publication Data available.

ISBN: 0-8118-4041-7

Manufactured in China

Designed by Tolleson Design / SF
Robata font designed by Kathryn Otoshi

Distributed in Canada by Raincoast Books
9050 Shaughnessy Street
Vancouver, British Columbia V6P 6E5

10 9 8 7 6 5 4 3 2 1

Chronicle Books LLC
85 Second Street
San Francisco, California 94105

www.chroniclebooks.com

CONTENTS

In his 1921 play R.U.R., Karel Čapek created the word "robot" from the Czech word robota, meaning "heavy labor."

As I watch my two young boys drawing spaceships and dinosaurs on the living room floor, I'm reminded of my first inspiration for *Robota*. I grew up in Michigan, where long winters and humid summers persuaded me to stay indoors and draw. I remember spending many hours after elementary school drawing robots. For me it was easier to *invent* friends than to make real ones.

One afternoon, I was doodling a sketch. It was more a scribble than a drawing, but something about the unfinished picture caught my attention. That image eventually became stuck in my brain and remained there for years. Why, I wouldn't understand until much later. That afternoon, I had sketched a picture of tall ships and flying saucers. It was my first drawing of Robota.

Flash forward to 1996.

I had just signed on to head up the art and design team for the new trilogy of *Star Wars* films. Inundated with more work than I could handle, I found the image of that unfinished drawing coming back to me. Perhaps it was a sign of the pressure I was under or simply a desire to recapture my youthful creativity. Whatever it was—maybe the odd juxtaposition of the two forms, complex versus simple, high tech versus low tech—the image of the flying saucers and tall ships resurfaced as if to remind me of unfinished work.

For the next year that image haunted me. A compelling story hid inside it, but I was already overcome with work and couldn't possibly take on another commitment to find it. Another year passed and the image remained. It was starting to become an obsession—one that couldn't wait the ten or more years I would need to finish my current responsibilities. Somehow I would need to find the time to work on it. *Perhaps at night after the kids are in bed or on weekends?*

Logic bypassed my brain. I was standing at the edge of a cliff thinking that if I stepped off, I would be okay. If I kept it a secret, no one would know if I failed. This seemed to assuage my fear. I gave myself an interim commitment of three months. Three months seemed reasonable. I could put up with anything for three months. I didn't realize then that the three months would grow to be three years, and that it was much harder *doing* something than *thinking* about doing it.

Nevertheless, once I had taken the first steps, I was determined to maintain the momentum. Even a snail's pace is *still* forward movement, and slowly the story elements came together.

I incorporated a scientific theory about a missing fourth planet of our solar system that, billions of years ago, collided with the proto-Earth to form our moon and enable life to germinate. This mythical fourth planet would be called Orpheus and become the setting for my story. In Greek mythology, the severed head of the poet Orpheus lived long after the death of his body. Life on Earth would be the legacy of Orpheus.

On my Orpheus, thousands of years before this collision, a race of benevolent sentient robots called the Olms came to warn the human population of their impending doom. They gave the preindustrial humans high technology, robot-building capabilities, and genetic engineering to save themselves. However, because of human frailties, the people of Orpheus lost sight of the original reason behind the gifts of knowledge and used the newly acquired technology to destroy themselves instead.

Then one day, as I was gathering *all* these ingredients, I realized—this is interesting material, but it's all background material. Where is the story? What I was developing was more historical than dramatic. It might as well have been an illustrated textbook on the history of Orpheus. I was stuck. I quieted my growing fear by telling myself that it was only a matter of time. But days, then weeks, passed and I was no closer to solving the story problem.

Fortunately, a family vacation forced me to put things aside, and I welcomed the change of pace. The beautiful drive down the coast of California was refreshing. On the road, my mind, no longer encumbered with self-imposed deadlines and expectations, wandered, and that's when something amazing happened . . .

All the jumbled pieces started to coalesce into plot points, characters, and motivations. I would set my story hundreds of years after the initial Olm visit. Even though this was an epic tale, it would be told as an intimate story of love, betrayal, and revenge. Still driving, I grabbed a pen and frantically scribbled notes on any scraps of paper I could find—a road map, hotel brochures, anything that could take a pen mark. I kept writing and driving. Fortunately, my wife is very good at steering from the passenger side! By the time we arrived at the hotel five hours later, I had a villain, a victim, a motive, and the story.

It would take another two years of writing and a fortuitous collaboration with Orson Scott Card to complete the work. Now, after nearly thirty years, that childhood sketch of flying saucers and tall ships is finally finished.

The story of *Robota* is born.

—Doug Chiang

PROLOGUE

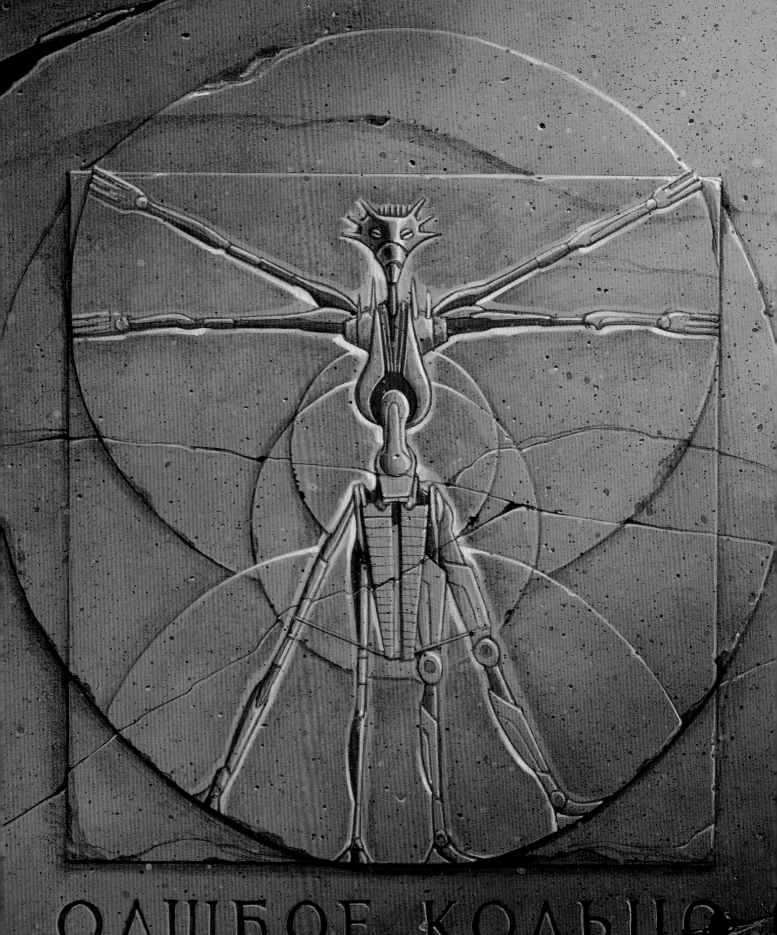

ОЛШБОЕ КОЛЬЦО

ROBOTA

Among the humans there is an ancient story of a hero laid out upon his deathbed, who rises up, slays his enemies, and then, when he is told that he was already dead, goes disappointed down into his grave.

There is a story among the robots, at least as ancient, of a human puppeteer who made a doll so lifelike that he treated it as his own daughter. He dressed her in the finest clothing he could afford to buy, and amassed such a dowry for her that there were many suitors who wanted the hand of his daughter in marriage. He granted the petition of one man, a very wealthy one, who took home the girl of wood and upholstery and seated her upon furniture made of the same stuff as she.

The doting father visited her every day, and all went well enough. The husband was relieved that the father never asked when his wooden child might become pregnant and give him grandchildren. The father was relieved that the husband seemed to have no other women in his life as rivals to the darling of his heart.

Worms got to her, though, and mildew, and all the rots and frays that organic life is prone to. At last, on one of his visits, the father came weeping to his son-in-law and told him that his daughter wanted to come home to die. The son-in-law joined him in grieving, and together they carried the girl back to the house where she had been carved and jointed, stitched and stuffed.

There the father nursed her, yet still she ailed, until one day he pronounced her dead and burned her body upon a pyre. Her widower came and wept, and when the fire had spent itself, he asked for her ashes and took them to his ancestral crypt, spreading them among the ashes of his ancestors and engraving her name upon the lintel stone beside the space where one day his own name would be carved.

The father loved his son-in-law then, for the honor he gave the daughter of his heart, and when he died he left all his fortune to his son-in-law, along with the secret of how to make a puppet live.

The robots tell this story as a jest, for to them the wooden puppet girl is more alive than the father or the husband, for anything that dies after so brief a span cannot truly be said ever to have been alive.

Humans learned this story from the robots, and they told it in their secret caves and hiding places. For centuries they told the tale, for to them it told a great poetic truth, that no device made by human hands is ever truly alive, and to treat it as if it lives is only sentimentality, or madness, or in the end, despair.

< 0.1 Stone Diagram

ROBOTA

The world once had another name, or rather a thousand other names, for every human language called it "earth," or "soil," or "home."

The most advanced of the humans had learned to harness wind, and they used it to drive ships upon the water and turn mill-wheels upon the land. They searched the coastlines and the open oceans of their world, and they navigated by sun and stars. They ground their grain and sawed their lumber, fed their growing millions of people, and thought themselves very modern and prosperous, far wiser than their ancestors.

> What tool can we imagine
> That we cannot make?
> We make the tools that
> make the tools that make
> the tools we use, and still
> we seek the tool to make all tools.
> Yet the tool to make all tools
> cannot be made.
> It must be found, and filled
> with wisdom, and then used.

So wrote a poet of the great age of sail. He published it, and it was widely read and translated (as part of a much longer — and very tedious — epic), and this stanza was known to the captain and even some of the sailors of the ship *Cloud of Hope*.

Cloud of Hope was almost in sight of shore when the first of the great robot starships appeared in the sky. It hovered like a bird that had caught an updraft, yet it had the sheen of pure silver. How could such a massive thing not fall into the sea?

Many sailors took it as a miracle, a manifestation of some god, and they prayed — some to appease whatever god sent it, and some to their own god, begging for protection.

The ship's surgeon took it as a madness born of long weeks at sea and the shortage of fresh vegetables, which caused the minds of weaker men to hallucinate after only a few days of deprivation.

The captain, however, as well as his artillery officer, thought of the poet's words, and they said to each other, "Someone has imagined this tool and has made it, and whoever has such power can only be our enemy. We must strike first, before it can strike us, so that we can flee this place and return home to warn our countrymen of this terrible enemy."

Or if they did not say those words, they said whatever words it took to induce them to load their cannons, tilt them upward as if they were mortars, and fire them almost directly overhead.

The first shot did not have enough powder, and it plummeted back down to the sea without ever touching the great robot starship. So vertical had been its trajectory that the *Cloud of Hope* almost sailed into its own shot, which splashed so close that it soaked a sailor who was furling the spritsail.

> 0.2 First Contact

0.3 The Olms Arrive

0.4   Air Battle

The second shot had plenty of powder, and when it struck the great ship, the clang of its impact rang like a distant bell.

"The thing is hollow," said the captain to his artillery officer.

"The thing is impervious to shot," said the artillery officer.

"More powder," said the captain.

"Flee," said the artillery officer.

But where could they flee? There was no place on earth where the starships did not come within the next few days and weeks.

And not one of the invaders was slain by any weapon of humankind.

For the invaders were machines, weren't they? And while they might be damaged or even destroyed, that which never lived can never die.

But humans can die, and therefore can fear death, and in fear of death can surrender. So for the hope of not dying, they gave over their freedom to the robots, and the world had a new name. Not "earth" or "soil" or "home," not one of those old names that spoke of life and hope and the mastery of humanity. The invaders named the place for themselves.

Robota.

Here is the irony: All the humans who surrendered to save their lives died anyway, after enough years had passed.

And if there was a time when humans thought they were happy living among their robot conquerors, it was out of madness. When the machine rules over the maker of machines, who then is the tool?

Or so the story was told among the humans during all the years of darkness.

< 0.5 Robot Conquerors

I

A SLEEP AND A FORGETTING

h e awoke from a dream of graceful wooden sailing ships, threatened by flying metal discs like saw blades whirling in the air. Yet it was also a dream of gentle voyagers returning home, bringing gifts to long-neglected friends.

He did not understand his own dream, or why it should have two meanings. Nor did he know where he was.

Inside a machine, that much he knew, but it was inscribed with symbols he did not understand, filled with levers and gauges whose purpose he did not know. He was wearing clothing that felt good on his body; he relished the sliding of the fabric across his skin. He was glad to be alive, and yet also weary and just a little bit afraid, though he did not know why.

As if it had detected his movement — for he touched nothing — part of the machine began to move, opening up and protruding an apparatus that quickly resolved itself into something that he knew at once was a face, though it did not resemble a human.

The machine spoke.

The voice, coming suddenly as it did, startled him so he did not listen at first, and when he began to pay attention, he found that although he understood most of the words, none of the sentences meant anything to him. What was Font Prime? What did the machine want him to do? It seemed as though the mes-sage might be instructions on how to do something, but he had no idea of the purpose or the process. It might as easily have been directions for a journey, but he had no idea of the destination or the route.

What has happened to me, he wondered, to leave me so ignorant of who I am or what I am supposed to do or why I'm in this place at all?

A shadow passed across a window of the machine. Someone was outside.

His first thought was to rush out and ask for explanations.

Then it occurred to him that not everything that could cast a shadow would be harmless, let alone friendly.

He looked for a weapon he might use to defend himself, but all he could find was what seemed to be a tool. It was not designed to kill

anything, but it was metal and would give greater force to any blow he might strike with his hand.

He unlatched the door and pushed. It opened easily, swinging up under its own power. Outside, the machine was surrounded by a grass meadow, which was rimmed by enormous trees. Climbing to the top of the machine, he looked around for the source of the shadow.

At that moment there burst from the forest a monstrous creature that must have been fifteen meters high. It pounded the ground with each footfall as it loped toward him.

"Run!" cried a shrill voice behind him.

He whirled to see who was speaking, only to have a monkey leap to his shoulders and screech again in his ear. "Run, you fool!"

The giant creature was almost upon him. Monkey on his shoulders, he leapt from the machine onto the grass and ran toward the trees.

The monster kept running, but it made no effort to follow him. Instead, it headed straight for the trees on the opposite side of the clearing from where it had entered.

The jodphur is running away, he thought.

And then he thought, How do I know it's called a jodphur?

A loud crack rang out. The huge creature stumbled, fell into a tree, then spun around in a slow, clumsy dance and fell to the ground, dead.

"Stay still," whispered the monkey on his shoulder. "Make no sound."

He stood in the shadows, hidden in the undergrowth, as the hunters came into the clearing. At first they were only shadows moving in the green shade of the trees. One of them smoked a pipe, as if he were out for a leisurely stroll rather than hunting monsters.

Then the hunters emerged into sunlight. They were not men at all. They were robots, carrying long thin rifles in their equally thin arms, moving on slender legs with the grace and precision of spiders.

R O B O T A

"Tinheads," whispered the monkey scornfully.

Even the one with a pipe was a robot.

How absurd. What pleasure could the fumes of a smoldering leaf bring to a mechanical mind?

The monkey began to tremble. "It's Kaantur-Set. He's going to find us, find us, find us."

"Quiet."

"He has a tool that lets him find us!" The monkey's voice rose in fear until it became a screech.

The smoking robot and several of the others turned their heads languidly toward him, and rifles began to shift in metal arms.

"Run!" cried the monkey.

But he was already running, the monkey clinging to his shoulders, his clothing, his hair. Behind him, he could hear the rhythmic pounding of the robots' feet as they bounded after him in perfect unison. Beat, beat, beat, beat. Closer, louder.

And before him the ground dropped away, three times deeper than the jodphur had been tall, steep as a wall. Before him stretched the walls and towers of an abandoned human city, overgrown with trees and vines, yet still splendid in its majesty. The nearest building was fifteen meters away, an ancient temple whose wall was shaped like a human face. No bridge spanned the gap. No man could jump so far.

The monkey leapt from his shoulders and scrambled down vines that clung to the face of the cliff. The man knew he would never be able to match the monkey's speed in climbing and would make too large a target, helpless as he descended.

The pounding of the robots' feet grew louder. He could hear them crashing through the undergrowth.

So he leapt.

He had no time to think of what he could or could not do; he simply jumped outward. He had no running start. He just pushed off with all the strength of his legs. As soon as he was in the air, he knew that he would die, for the drop was too far for a man to fall and still live.

But he did not hit the ground. Instead he slammed into the parapet atop the temple on the far side of the chasm.

He had no time to wonder how he could have leapt so far. He had to get over the parapet and behind the massive tree that grew atop the sculpted head like a spear that had pierced it.

As he scrambled upward, the ancient, moss-eaten stone crumbled under his hands and feet. He slid. He fell, bumping against the

< **1.5** Kaantur, the Hunter

nose and then crashing onto bare stone at the temple's base.

He must have been dazed by the fall, for by the time he was able to raise his head from the ground and look around, two robots were already upon him, pointing their rifles at him.

But they did not shoot. Waiting? For the one with the pipe? The one the monkey had called Kaantur-Set?

Was there some way to escape? I am stronger than I imagined possible, he thought, to have made the leap I made. Yet these robots must have strength beyond anything a human's bones could support. Strength and quickness and accuracy. I couldn't run away quickly enough; fighting them would be useless; yet to lie here and die . . .

Suddenly a tall shape moved into view behind the robots, silhouetted by the sun behind it. Something sinuous in its movements told him this newcomer was alive, not a machine. Not a jodphur this time. Rapidly it moved toward the robots and, with huge hands, struck blows that knocked the weapons from their grips. The hunter-beast picked up one robot, then the other, and broke them like branches.

‹ 1.6 The Leap / 1.7 No Escape

Without showing a sign that he had even seen the man, the hunter-beast bent over and pried the antennae from the robots he had just broken.

The hunter-beast wore an apparatus on its head that covered its ears and had a thin rod that extended near its mouth. A headset, the man realized. So it can hear. And speak. It has language.

"Thank you," said the man.

"This is no place for humans," answered the hunter-beast.

Of course it could speak. Like the monkey, hadn't it been bred partly from human genes? A robot-killer that could handle enemies that ordinary humans could not fight?

Why do I know this, and yet so little else?

"Tinheads kill any animal they find," said the hunter-beast.

"What's your name?" asked the man.

"Juomes," said the hunter-beast. "What's yours?"

He could not answer because, of course, he did not know. "There were robots behind me, up on top of the cliff."

"Then soon they'll be down here," said Juomes. "When they get the trail of a human, they never give up." Trophies in hand, Juomes turned and climbed onto a large flea-like creature.

"Don't leave me," said the man. "I don't know where I am or where to go."

Juomes barely paused. "When they follow you, I don't want them to find *me*. Rend will lead you."

"Rend?" said the man to Juomes's back. And then the hunter-beast was gone.

At once the monkey leapt from a low branch and scampered along the foot of the temple wall.

"I'm Rend, you fool!" cried the monkey. "Don't you remember anything? They're coming, they're going to find you, follow me! Follow me, Caps!"

"Is that my name?" asked the man.

"It is until they kill you because you're too stupid to move out of this clearing!" screeched Rend.

Caps followed him into dark low paths among the trees, winding upward, around the steep cliff that Caps had jumped. "You know me, then?" he asked.

"We go through this every time," said Rend. "Don't you learn anything?"

"I don't remember ever doing this before," said Caps.

◁ **1.8** Juomes and the Robots

"Well, I can promise you I don't plan to do it again," said Rend.

"Take me back to the machine I came out of," said Caps. "Where you found me. There must be something there that will tell me what I'm supposed to do. Maybe it'll play the message it played before, and you can listen to it and help me understand it."

Rend leapt up and dangled from a branch before his face. "I don't go in there," said Rend. "You're on your own."

Rend pointed the way for Caps to go, then swung up into the higher branches, calling down as he climbed, "You're on your own now!"

Moving as quickly as he could in the direction Rend had pointed, Caps soon emerged into the clearing where his machine had been. But it was not there.

It had been dragged away from the clearing. Since the machine was large and heavy, Caps was not eager to meet whatever it was that had moved it. Yet if he was to find out more about who he was and what he was supposed to do, he had no choice but to follow its path into the forest.

Caps might have the ability to leap across chasms, but that did not make him good at stealth in the woods. He did not see the hunter robot until he was almost upon him.

This robot was not quite like the others — he was marked with orange on his right arm, though what the marking meant Caps could not guess. And instead of pointing his weapon at him, the robot merely gestured harshly for him to leave.

But he did not speak. Because he could not? Or because he did not want to be heard?

When Caps did not obey, the hunter shook his head and then ran off into the woods.

Caps looked around to see if the hunter was warning him of something. But how far could he see into the underbrush? He looked up into the branches of a tree and saw nothing there, either.

And yet his eyes kept returning to one spot, as if some deep part of his brain recognized something that his conscious mind did not. He studied the place, and gradually came to realize that, even though it was very still, there was something alive perched among the branches.

Alive, not a robot. Even before he realized it was a human, he knew it was not a machine.

As he stared, the figure moved, emerging from its hidden posture to stand openly on a heavy branch. It was a young woman, luminous with beauty, wearing ragtag clothing that, astonishingly, was white. How had she managed to remain concealed? Why would she wear white in a place where robots were hunting? She seemed to have ample reason for confidence, judging from the robot-antenna trophies she wore on her belt.

Why is she watching me? Or was she watching the hunter robot? Did I spoil her kill? Or . . .

Before he could speculate further, Rend burst screeching from the woods, soaring three meters over Caps's head. "I found your nest!" he cried. "But the hunters found *me!*"

Caps did not wait to see how close behind Rend the hunter robots were. He followed him into the woods, and the chase was on again.

Rend knew where he was going, and Caps did not, so this time Caps followed him faithfully. Soon they were back at the temple ruins, and Rend flung himself into a shadow that did not look like an opening.

As he dropped to the ground and slid into the opening, Caps realized that it still didn't look like an opening, or not much of one. The robots were more slender than any adult human — they could go through any aperture Caps could fit through. But what made this passage a good escape was that it bent almost immediately between stones, first to the right, then down, then left, then up, then out, in turns so tight that Caps had to contort himself in ways he had not imagined possible in order to fit.

Robots might be stronger and quicker and thinner than humans, but their joints weren't as flexible and their skin had no give to it. This was one of the few places where a man could go and a robot couldn't.

Caps wondered, briefly, if that's precisely why this passageway was built.

1.11 The Encounter and the Warning

But how could it have been? This temple dated from the glorious days when robot and human were still friends, living together, co-operating, learning from each other.

How do I know that? wondered Caps yet again.

In the darkness he bumped into something hairy.

"Rend?" asked Caps.

"Up or down?" asked Rend.

"How should I know? You're the one who knows the passageways, not me."

"I only come here to hide from predators. I wait till they go away or fall asleep. But Kaantur-Set will post a watch. Robots never sleep. Robots never disobey."

Caps thought of the orange-marked robot and wondered.

Outside the passageway, they could hear a harsh voice reprimanding the hunters. "You had him in your sights. You didn't fire. Why?"

Caps heard no reply. Then a single gunshot suggested there would never be a reply.

Again the harsh voice. "And you? Where were you?"

"I thought I saw him in the trees."

Could this be the orange-marked robot?

"Thought?"

"I saw something, and thought that it was him."

"I should shoot you, too."

"If I deserve it, you will," said the robot.

"Stand guard, and shoot any beast or man that comes out of that hole," said Kaantur-Set. "I will also have a guard stand watch on you, from up there, where you can't see."

Could it be the orange-marked robot? Kaantur-Set had not killed him, but he did not fully trust him, either. Had the orange-marked robot been trying to save Caps's life by motioning him to leave?

Don't try to find explanations alone in the dark, Caps told himself.

"Up or down?" Caps asked Rend.

"I asked you first," said Rend.

"Down, then."

This passageway was much smoother, and instead of sharp angles it had gentle curves and bends.

Then a stone rocked downward and sent Caps and Rend slipping down a steep slide. They didn't stop until they became entangled in a net, which swung out to dangle in the middle of a dimly lit room.

"I think this is a trap," said Rend.

"But not an ancient one," said Caps. "Because this net is new."

"You smell like a human," said Rend, sniffing disdainfully.

"I'm allergic to monkey fur," said Caps.

"I thought you didn't remember anything," said Rend.

"I didn't remember it. I discovered it," said Caps.

The room had once been ceremonial. The walls were painted with heroic-sized depictions of humans and robots engaged in solemn activities together. But all around the room, shelves and tables had been put up, many of them makeshift contraptions that could barely support their contents.

What they held were a few books, a lot of papers in haphazard-looking stacks, and bottles, jars, vials, boxes, tubes, trays, dishes, and a weird assortment of once-living things — heads and other body parts of various animals, lots of different leaves and roots, and hundreds of herbs growing in pots placed along the one wall, which would presumably be scanned by sunlight from the high windows during the course of the day.

Specimens. Whoever used this room was a biologist. This was a laboratory.

Then they heard the grinding sound of stone rolling across stone, and they fell silent, waiting to see who their captor was.

It was the hunter-beast Juomes, who had saved him after he fell. Juomes moved about slowly, taking off his trophies and weapons, putting them away, giving no sign that he saw that his net was full. Neither Caps nor Rend felt any need to break the silence.

"Got away from the tinheads," said Juomes at last, chuckling, "and came to visit me."

He lowered the net to the ground and unfastened it at the top. Rend immediately scampered away, running for safety, hiding somewhere. Caps didn't have that option.

Instead he studied his . . . what, captor? Deliverer? He noticed that on a jewel that hung on a chain around Juomes's neck, there was inscribed a symbol Caps had seen inside the machine where he awoke. The symbol had no meaning to him, but he thought it significant that Juomes voluntarily wore something that might be connected to the machine. It did not prove him to be either friend or foe. It was simply a fact, which Caps would remember and try to make sense of. If there was some link to the machine, there was a chance Juomes would know something to help Caps understand who he was and what had happened to his memory.

> **1.12** Juomes

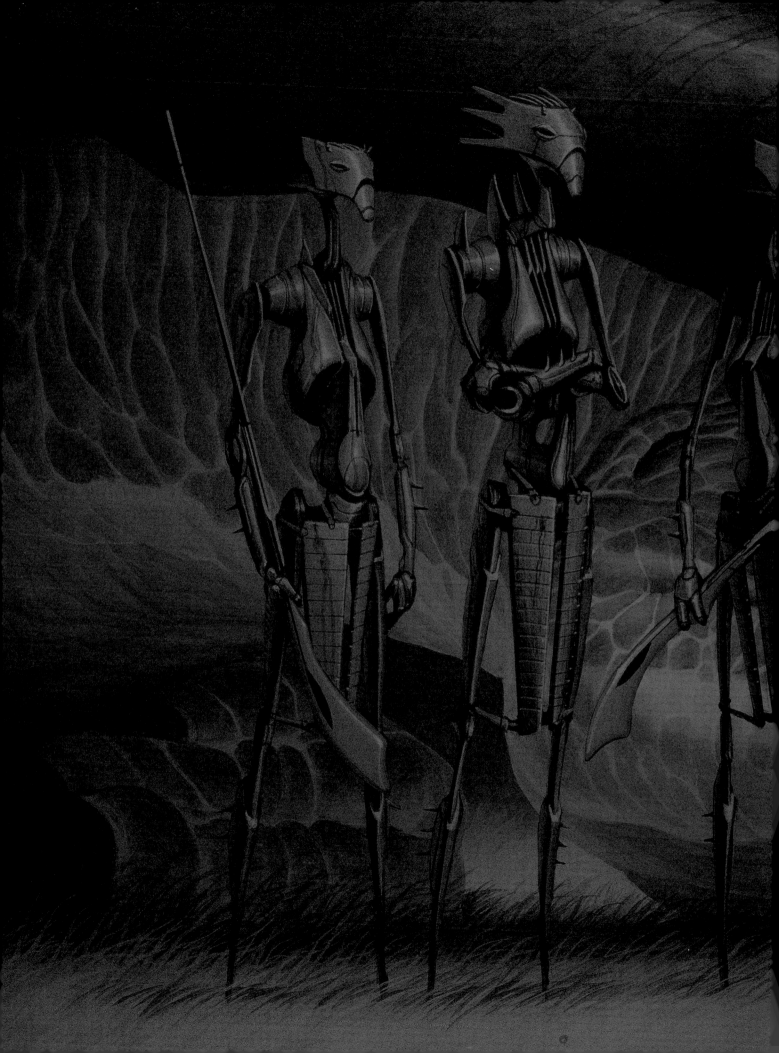

II

THE HAND OF JUOMES

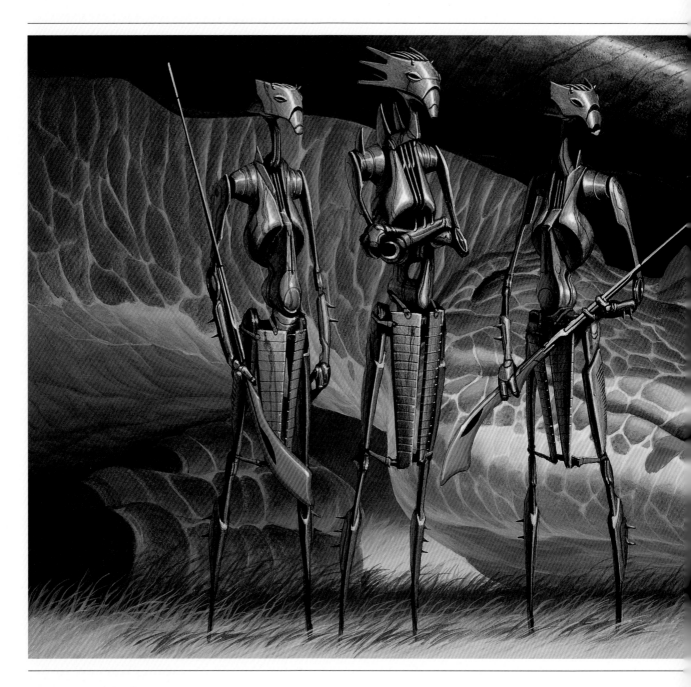

2.1 Portrait of the Hunters

But it was Juomes who asked the questions, not Caps, and when he learned of the machine, he insisted that Caps and Rend lead him there. Once they got him in the vicinity, Juomes took the lead, sniffing the air and holding still, listening and watching carefully, and then moving branches slowly so that the three of them made no sound as they passed through the underbrush to a good vantage point.

The robots had webbed the machine with cables and were hitching it to several large beasts. Apparently they meant to haul it some-where — probably to a road. Caps thought it ironic that the robots had to resort to the labor of beasts when a really difficult task was at hand. Later, when he said as much to Juomes, the hunter-beast spat and said, "They have no problem with domesticated animals. If *we* were tame and they could use us as tools, they'd not kill us, either."

Now, though, watching the robots at work, they said nothing.

A plume of smoke announced that Kaantur-Set was emerging from the machine. Caps felt an irrational anger that this man-imitating robot had been inside *his* place — though in truth Caps had no idea if the place was really his. For all he knew, he had been put there by an enemy, who used the machine to wipe out his memories.

But if that was so, what was the incomprehensible message about?

And now that he thought about it, the facelike image that delivered the message resembled these hunter robots. For all Caps knew, the machine really did belong to them, and he was just a dumb animal who had stumbled into it and pulled the wrong lever.

Kaantur-Set followed the smoke of his pipe out of the machine.

Caps now had a chance to look at him without running away, and he saw something else. A preserved animal paw hung from around Kaantur-Set's waist. A talisman?

A trophy. Like the antennae that Juomes and that woman collected and wore around their waists.

Juomes started breathing heavily and rushed away. Caps and Rend followed. As soon as they were far enough from the robots to dare to speak, Caps asked him what was wrong. Juomes didn't explain, but said they had to get back to his hideout.

The place was in a shambles. Someone had ransacked it. "I only have one thing worth stealing," he said. "My jewel."

Sure enough, it was gone.

"I thought you wore it," said Caps.

"Not when I was heading for your machine," said Juomes. "I feared a trap. Better they should kill me than take the jewel."

"But they've taken it anyway," said Rend.

"Yes," said Juomes bitterly, knocking boxes and papers aside in vain. "It *was* a trap, but a more subtle one than I expected."

"It suggests they knew you had this jewel," said Caps, "and knew where you lived, and watched you and waited until you were out."

"They'll be back," said Rend.

"Of course," said Juomes. "But what do I care?"

He pulled the battle glove from his left hand. Under it was a prosthetic hand.

"Looks like you're part robot," said Rend.

Juomes casually batted him across the room with the back of his right hand. Rend rolled away, cursing, unhurt.

"That was your hand at Kaantur-Set's belt, wasn't it?" said Caps.

"He took my hand trying to get me to give him my jewel," said Juomes. "After he killed my family, he thought that taking my hand would make me confess?" Juomes laughed bitterly. "Now he has the jewel anyway."

"Why would he want it?" asked Caps.

"These jewels with the symbol on them came from an ancient spaceship. They allowed the higher animals to 'cube' — to become intelligent, to speak. Like our monkey friend here."

"No jewel made *me* smart," said Rend.

"How did it work?" asked Caps.

"I'm not a scientist," said Juomes. "Are you?"

"I just — did they eat the jewel or wear it to sleep or what?" asked Caps.

"It hasn't worked in years," said Rend, "or Juomes wouldn't be so stupid."

Juomes ignored him. "Once it changes an animal, it breeds true — all its offspring have speech as well. It brought a golden age to the world. It made the robots jealous, and the king of the robots, Font Prime, sent out Kaantur-Set and his hunters to destroy all the jewels. They think when the jewels are gone, we'll all become dumb beasts again. Mine was the last."

"Font Prime," said Caps.

"Do you remember something?" asked Rend eagerly.

"The message inside my machine. It mentioned Font Prime."

"I'm going to find Font Prime," said Juomes. "I'm going to kill it. That will end the persecution of the animals."

"I'll go with you," said Caps, "if you'll have me."

"To help me?"

"I don't know if you need my help," said Caps. "A man with no memory."

"Oh, you have a memory," said Juomes. "You know how to speak. How to reason. You know many things. All that you've forgotten is yourself."

"He forgot me, too," said Rend.

"Everyone who knows you tries to forget you," said Juomes.

"But they all fail," said Rend smugly.

"Come with me, Caps," said Juomes. "I'll teach you to fight. Maybe your memories will come back to you. Maybe you know something, locked in your head, something that will lead me to my jewel, or if I can't save it now, then to Font Prime."

III

THE CUBING JEWEL

3.1 Desert Rocks / 3.2 Seashore

3.3 Bilellepad Robot Factory / 3.4 Desert Shore

When the children of the hunter-beasts tell the story, Juomes is the hero — and who can blame them? In their tale, Caps was like a baby, and Juomes taught him everything.

Juomes did teach him, talking to him as they journeyed by day. And when they stopped at night for sleep, and when they first arose in the morning, he tried to teach Caps to fight.

Juomes discovered that Caps had strength and adroitness beyond any mere teaching, however. Juomes had only to show Caps how to do a maneuver with a weapon or with his bare hands, and Caps mastered it at once. And when they sparred, weapon on weapon, Caps could disarm the great hunter-beast by brute strength alone.

"You don't look it," said Juomes, "but you were born to be the scourge of the robots."

Rend was not impressed. "Big animals fighting to see who's strongest. Monkey goes where they can't go, monkey sees what they can't see."

"Monkey poops and throws it at big animals," said Juomes.

"I can also pee in their eyes," said Rend. "Everybody does what he can do."

They followed the robots through grassland, desert, along the shores of the sea. The trail of the machine was unmistakable, for it was

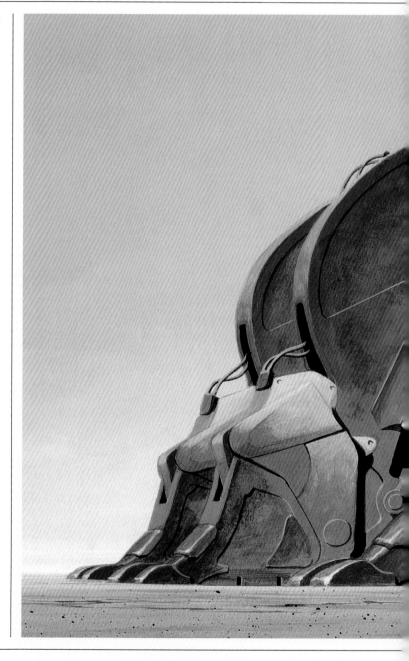

3.5 Midday Rest and a Lesson

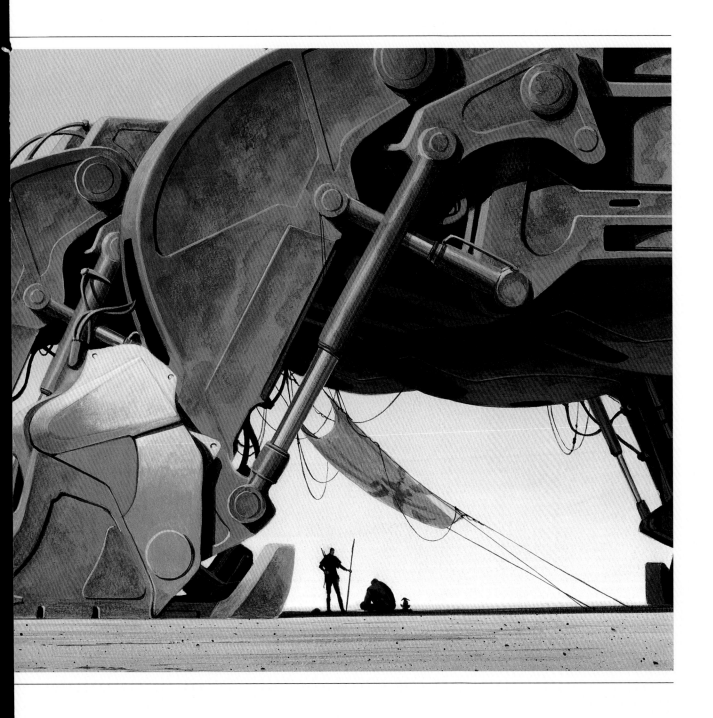

3.6 Robot Encampment

ROBOTA

either dragged through narrow places or slung between four heavy-footed beasts in open country.

Here is the most important thing Juomes told Caps as they traveled:

"The robots are afraid. Each one we kill is irreplaceable, because they've lost the ability to reproduce themselves."

Caps was confused. "How can a machine not make another machine? They should have great factories that churn them out, thousands in a day."

Juomes looked at him oddly. "You see what I mean? You remember another world, another time — it's only this day and age that you have forgotten. No, they make the robots all right, but they're only empty shells. Machines that do nothing but what they're commanded to do. That's the other reason they want the cubing jewels. But they won't work. The jewels turn living things sentient. Those robots are dead from the start."

"How could they forget how to make new robots? Was there some secret that they've forgotten?"

"Am I a robot?" asked Juomes. "I know that much and no more. And if I knew more I wouldn't tell. The robots don't replace their dead? Good. Let that continue till the last one is dead. Then, if any sentient animals survive, the world is ours. Never to be called 'Robota' again."

It made Caps uneasy to hear such talk, though he didn't know why, not then.

They overtook Kaantur-Set's robots near the rusting hulk of an old drilling machine. The robots seemed not to notice that they were being followed, and for their part, Juomes and Caps and Rend could not see any plausible way to get the jewel from them. Robots did not sleep; they only camped because the beasts pulling the machine had to rest. They would be alert all night. "In the forest we might take one or two in the darkness," whispered Juomes. "Here is their element — a bare place without life. We'll watch. We'll follow."

The robots led them to the ruins of a city. The buildings were huge, but still dwarfed by thousand-foot trees that had grown in the years since the city was abandoned. Robot guards were stationed at the gate. Juomes led Caps and Rend by another way. It involved a lot of climbing, but they were strong and it was exhilarating to take possession of such a place.

"It was built by humans?" asked Caps.

"Robots don't need cities. They don't need rooms like these. They don't need beauty. When you're done with robots you can stack them up like stones. Only animals like us need dens. Only cubed animals need their dens to be beautiful."

An avalanche had thrown huge boulders into one edge of the city, and it was among these

> 3.7 Ruins in the Trees

3.8 Elyseo's Fate

giant stones that Rend discovered a robot's head. He brought the others to see it.

"Help," said the head.

"Where are your friends?" said Juomes sarcastically.

"They took me apart to rust when the rains come," said the head. "Because I refused to hunt."

"Hunt what?"

"You," said the head. "Kaantur-Set ordered me to go back and kill you."

"Back away," said Juomes to the others. "He's been wired as a bomb."

"I was," said the head, "but I recircuited myself. I'm harmless now. Look, the explosives are tucked into my skull at the base. They were set to go off when you kicked me or rolled me."

"It's a trap," said Juomes.

Caps walked over and picked up the head. Nothing exploded.

"Thanks for trusting me," said the head.

"You're insane," said Juomes.

"I know this one," said Caps. "He tried to save me."

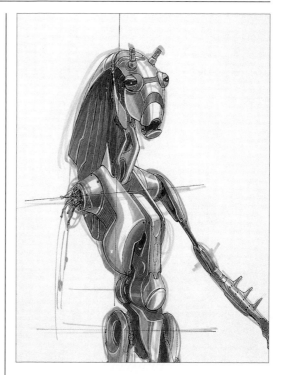

"Everybody tries to save you," said Juomes, "and still you go on trying to get killed."

"Where is the rest of your body?" Caps asked the robot.

Juomes asked in disbelief. "You're not going to put him back together, are you?"

"I'll understand if you refuse to let me travel with you," said Caps. "But this robot is not like the others. He doesn't kill animals. So he doesn't deserve to die."

"They all kill animals," said Juomes.

3.9 Elyseo-Set

"A robot that Kaantur-Set wanted to kill," said Caps, "is a tool we might have a use for."

"He knew we'd find him," said Juomes.

"But he didn't know we'd put it back together," said Caps.

"Do you two mind if I set off these explosives?" said Rend. "They'll be expecting to hear a big boom, and we shouldn't disappoint them." He sounded eager.

"The monkey likes bombs," said Juomes.

"Not till I find all the parts," said Caps.

Rend helped, though Juomes didn't, and finally they had everything except one arm. With the head directing him, Caps put the robot back together until the robot was able to reassemble the rest of himself without help.

"Every robot life is precious these days," said the one-armed robot. "My name is Elyseo-Set."

Juomes snorted. "A talking machine doesn't need a name."

"I'm Caps," said Caps.

There was a loud explosion not very far away. It momentarily deafened Caps, and by the time he could hear again Rend came scampering back.

"It was a big one!" he screeched. Then he looked around, as if trying to find the sound of his own voice. "I sound far away, but here I am!"

By a waterfall, Kaantur-Set heard the explosion. "They took the bait," he said to his hunters.

He threw Elyseo's arm into the water.

⠿⠿⠿⠿⠿⠿⠿⠿⠿⠿⠿⠿

"You're the man who was in the teleporter, aren't you?" said Elyseo to Caps. "General Kaantur-Set, the great and wise — and he almost kills you out of habit."

"Teleporter?" said Caps.

"No such thing," said Juomes. "An old legend. If they could teleport, why would they need to make such a long journey of it?"

Rend, who was apparently reading lips, jumped up and down and said, "Can they put a teleporter inside itself?"

"The teleporters worked for humans," said Elyseo. "When the humans left the cities and turned wild, we robots could not make the machines teleport for us."

"You mean when the robots expelled us!" said Juomes.

3.10 Kaantur's Stiltwalker

Elyseo looked at Juomes. "*You* were never expelled," he said. "*Your* kind didn't exist then. That's how long ago it was."

The hunter-beasts had come into existence after the humans left these great cities? Caps could make no sense of it. How did the cubing jewels fit into this version of the past? Yet robot memories did not forget as animals did, substituting false information for true. What memories robots lost simply disappeared. So either Elyseo was lying or he never knew the truth, or the cubing jewels had come to the animals after humans and robots had separated.

Why do I want so badly to learn the truth of this? wondered Caps. What can it possibly matter to me?

They emerged from the other side of the city into thick viny forest. Desert on one side of the city, jungle on the other. The city was huge, but the climate difference had to do with the great mountains behind the city, which forced the rain to fall almost exclusively on the leeward side.

In late afternoon they began to make camp in a fairly open grove of trees. They were arguing about whether it was safe to sleep with Elyseo among them when some of the trees began to move.

It was jodphurs, their faces covered with battlepaint, that broke from the trees, and the party was surrounded.

3.11 Surrounded

IV

THE TAME AND THE WILD

"They're tame," said Caps.

"How can you call them tame?" said Elyseo. "They've taken us captive."

"They aren't eating us," said Caps.

"I know them," said Juomes. "They wouldn't have taken us, except we have that machine with us."

"Who are they, then?" said Caps.

"They aren't tame," said Juomes. "They've cubed."

"Jodphurs?" said Elyseo. "Impossible."

"Look at their heads. At what's attached at their ears. Translators. You don't do that with tame animals. You only do that with creatures that can speak."

"So they can understand us?" asked Caps.

The jodphur carrying him roared. Immediately afterward, a tinny voice from its translator said, "Yes, you fool."

"From a roar, the translator got *that*?" said Caps.

"From the roar, the translator got 'you fool.' The 'yes' came directly from its brain," said Juomes.

⟨ **4.1** Jodphur Commander

"That sounds suspiciously like robotics," said Elyseo.

"When there's a living mind telling the machine what to do, it's not a robot," said Juomes. "Where there's life, then the machine remains a tool."

"So a fungus with a stick is better than Font Prime?" asked Elyseo.

"Probably not better at mathematics," said Caps. No one was amused.

The jodphurs took them to a city — the kind that humans lived in now. In a forest of immense mushrooms, human workers had carved hundreds of rooms into the stalks and caps.

"How do mushrooms grow so big?" asked Caps.

"Because humans wanted them to," said Juomes.

"Have the mushrooms cubed?" asked Elyseo.

"When you're disassembled again," said Juomes, "and your parts are melted down to slag, remember that even jodphurs can cube, but you can't."

For Caps, though, the real question remained. "Why haven't the robots found this place?"

4.2 The Hidden City of the Jodphurs

ROBOTA

4.3　Keedim the Elder

"There are many mushrooms," said Juomes, "and only one of them, at any particular time, is a city."

The jodphurs deposited them at last before a group of elders of the human city. Caps was relieved to see other people built to the same scale he was. There were also elders of the jodphurs with them.

"Except that you had a robot with you, you would have been brought here as guests instead of prisoners," said Eyth, an old woman who was most senior of the human elders.

The leader of the jodphurs, Keedim, sniffed Caps's face like an enormous dog. "You have been seen before," said the mechanical voice from his headset. "You have killed no living creature."

"I've eaten fruits whenever I could find them," said Caps. "I can't vouch for the origin of what Juomes has fed us."

Keedim laughed — a terrifying thing, when a jodphur laughs. "My old friend Juomes. What are you doing with a whole robot, instead of just taking his antennae?"

"It was this human's idea," said Juomes.

Caps explained, then, how Elyseo had warned them his head was booby-trapped. "And earlier," said Caps, "he tried to warn me that Kaantur-Set was coming. He has no use for Kaantur's campaign against the living."

4.4 Transept City Gate Keeper

"A robot that doesn't serve Font Prime?" asked Eyth.

"Font Prime has not been seen in centuries," said Elyseo. "All we see is Kaantur. For all I know, Kaantur has destroyed Font Prime. Or cut him off from all its machinery, so he can't talk to any of us but him."

"That's what they want us to believe," said a younger voice.

She stepped out from among the elders — the young woman Caps had seen back in the forest.

"You," he said. "You saw how Elyseo tried to save me."

"I saw a robot waving his arms," said the young woman. "What he meant to do, and whether he was this robot, I can't say."

"Juomes, you're an honest man," said Caps. "Tell them —"

Caps was interrupted by the laughter of the elders, for Juomes was acting comically offended by having been called a man.

"I am a hunter-beast," he said.

"An honest one," Caps persisted. "Once he was reassembled, Elyseo could have betrayed us at any time."

"How do we know he didn't?" said Juomes. "How do we know he hasn't used *these*" —

and he tweaked Elyseo's antennae — "to tell Kaantur-Set where we are?"

"I think the more important question," said the young woman to Caps, "is who *you* are, and why we should trust *you*."

"Are you one of the elders?" asked Caps. "You seem young."

The woman looked at him with cool disdain, as if to say, I may seem young, but I know more than you do.

"Beryl is the one who brought us news of you," said Eyth.

"She is the one who kept us from killing you when we saw you," said Keedim.

"The machine you've been following," said Beryl. "The one that apparently spawned *you* — Kaantur and his hunters took it to Transept City."

"Then you'll never get it back," said Elyseo. "The Guardians of Transept City are far fiercer than the hunter robots. They aren't sentient, but they're relentless and irresistibly powerful. Not even a jodphur could stand against them."

"Silence that thing," said Keedim.

Two jodphurs lifted Elyseo by his legs and dangled him high above them, ready to smash him to the ground and grind him underfoot, if given the word.

"There was a monkey with them," said Beryl.

"Jodphurs can't catch monkeys," said Juomes. "Except in the sense that dogs catch fleas."

That was all it took to bring Rend out of hiding. He had clung to the nearly nerveless spine of the last of the jodphurs through the journey. Now he came out scolding Juomes, even though his own method of arrival seemed to illustrate just what Juomes had said.

Everyone laughed at this, but in the end, their questioning turned serious again. Where did you come by the name Caps? I don't know, Rend told me that was my name and I knew of no other. How did you come to be inside a teleporter — if that's what it is? I don't know. Rend said that every time I tried to use it, I came out with no memory. Then how do you know language, and all the other things you seem to know? I told you, I don't remember, I have no idea. I am what you see before you.

"I can't find out who I am without finding out how that machine brought me here, and where I came from. So if you let me go, I'll make my way to Transept City and try to learn what I can."

"Then you'll be killed," said Keedim. "Your pet robot is right in saying that no humans — or jodphurs, or hunter-beasts — have come out of there alive."

"I'm going with him," said Juomes. "They have my jewel now. I want it back."

"That's not all you want," said Beryl, challenging him.

"All right then," Juomes answered. "I'm tired of this game. The robots will die out eventually, since they can make no more. But it's taking too long."

Keedim smiled grimly. "You seem to have no faith in the work *we're* doing."

"Maybe you'll succeed, maybe you won't," said Juomes. "Meanwhile, I'll find Font Prime, if I can, and when I do, I'll destroy it."

"And you trust this stranger, this 'Caps,' on such a dangerous mission?" said Keedim.

"We have already trusted each other," said Juomes. "There's more to him than meets the eye."

"Go, then," said Eyth. "We won't keep you. But the robot stays, to be tried for his crimes."

Caps laughed. "Tried? For his crimes? When your only conceivable witness claims she can't tell one robot from another? And how can a machine commit a crime? All you'd be doing is trying him for the crimes of other robots."

They looked at him in silence. "A citizen of our city could be expelled for saying such things," said Eyth.

> 4.5 Beryl, the Eyes of the Forest

"Then you're no better than Kaantur-Set," said Caps. "He also sentenced Elyseo to die because of things he said."

"You test our patience," said Keedim. "I need no trial. I will throw this robot to the ground and grind it under my feet."

"Do that and you will have sentenced Juomes and me to death," said Caps, "because Elyseo is our only hope of accomplishing our mission in Transept City."

"What?" said Juomes. "I would never trust a machine!"

"You have no choice," said Caps. "It's a robot city. Do you know where anything is? Do you think they post directories of the city in convenient places for visitors to read? We have no hope without a guide, and we have no guide but Elyseo."

It took another half hour, but the jodphurs set Elyseo down — none too gently — and Eyth and Keedim agreed that he could go with Caps and Juomes.

"Then I'm going, too," announced Beryl.

"Why?" asked Caps.

"Because I have also been in Transept City," said Beryl. "Not far, but far enough to know about the Guardians. And to have evaded them and escaped. Up to a point, I'll know if the robot leads us true."

"If 'Beryl the Eyes of the Forest' wants to be the eyes of the city as well," said Juomes, "I'm glad to have her with us."

Thus it was that, in the morning, it was a party of five that set off for Transept City: Caps, Juomes, Beryl, Rend, and Elyseo. Through the forest of mushrooms Beryl led the way.

"How did humans make such mushrooms grow?" asked Caps.

"We have given up the science of tools — we can never defeat the robots using machines," said Beryl. "But the science of life, we excel at that. Let us say that we taught a mushroom to do what no mushroom had ever done, and when its spores sprouted, the new-sprung mushrooms remembered the lessons better than their parents."

"So was it your science of life that brought intelligence to the jodphurs?" asked Caps.

"It was my jewel," said Juomes. "It belonged to my grandmother, and she lent it to the people of the city. Wasn't it?"

Beryl only smiled. "What kind of fool would try to bring intelligence to the most dangerous predator in the world?"

"I'd say Kaantur-Set's hunters are the most dangerous," said Caps.

"They aren't predators," said Beryl. "They're a disease."

4.6 - 4.10 Creatures of the Forest

‹ **4.11** Caps and Rend / **4.12** Painted

"And maybe," said Juomes, "we're the cure."

Caps remembered something Keedim had said. "What is the work they're doing — your people, I mean, Beryl?"

"We stay alive," she said. "We find ways to farm that won't be obvious, so we can feed our people. We try to protect our children from the robots, so there'll be a next generation."

"But when Keedim said Juomes had no faith in the work your people were doing, they were talking about the decline of the robots, and how long it was taking."

"What are you talking about?" asked Juomes, as if Caps were crazy.

"You certainly trust in your memory," said Beryl, "considering that it only works intermittently."

Only then did Caps realize that whatever the work of the human mushroom city might be, they weren't going to tell him, at least not in front of Elyseo. And even if Elyseo were not there, they still might not trust Caps enough to tell him anything that really mattered. Caps couldn't blame them. He didn't even know himself well enough to know if he could be trusted.

4.13 Rock City

V

CITIES OF STONE AND AIR

<< **5.1** Strangers and Friends / **5.2** Stone and Air

There are versions of the legend in which this noble party entered Transept City accompanied by a great windstorm that filled the city with sand and dust, or an earthquake that opened a gate for them, or a flood that made rivers of the streets.

In reality they entered the city like awestruck tourists. The gates were not barred or even supervised. Nor had anyone accosted them as they approached, passing great stone shapes that seemed to be a mockery of the mushroom city, except that some of them still hung in the air, suspended by the gravity balancers of some ancient sculptor. They also passed the fallen heads of statues once built in memory of robots — though Juomes insisted that the robots had been gargoyles. "There's no point building statues of machines. They all look alike."

Transept City had been carved out of a great pillar of stone. It was a city built for giants, but it stood so high above the surrounding terrain that the vast scale of it could not be seen. Robots entered and left the city by means of shafts and elevators.

The five legendary heroes climbed up by means of one of the old construction ramps that wound around and around the shaft of the pillar. To Caps's surprise, it was Juomes who called for a rest now and then. Though he claimed he was stopping out of concern for Beryl and Rend, neither of them ever seemed tired, and Juomes always did. But

5.3 Transept City

ROBOTA

no one said anything about it. It occurred to Caps that, while Juomes had begun the journey full of vigor, seemingly inexhaustible, the rigors of the trip were taking a heavy toll on him. He seemed to require more effort to start moving, like an old man or a machine that needed oiling. Well, he might *be* old.

Apart from the sheer effort of going end-lessly uphill, though, the passage into the city was easy, with neither obstacle nor challenge. Juomes must have been thinking the same thing, because he said to Beryl, "Now that I see how easy it is, I'm a little less impressed that you were able to get inside."

"It was getting out that presented the main challenge," she replied.

Here's how heroic they were: They followed Elyseo into the city, ignoring his protest that the Guardians would sense them immediately. He led them in and out of passageways and chambers, vast empty things. But they never moved as fast as he urged them to, because they could not help but gawk at the sheer size of everything around them. Even Juomes, large as he was, looked like a baby playing in his parents' closet.

"Now you know how *I* feel all the time," said Rend.

That was their last laugh inside Transept City, for as they rounded the next corner they found themselves facing a half dozen

5.4 The Guardians of Transept City

ROBOTA

Guardians, huge white machines more than ten meters high, which strode on two legs and outran them in moments when they tried to flee.

To Caps's surprise, however, the Guardians did not kill them or even hurt them — their grasp was considerably gentler than the jodphurs' had been.

"They're designed to catch, not to kill," said Elyseo.

"So what happens to us?"

"They junk us," said Elyseo. "We're assumed to be defective robots."

The Guardians lowered them into a giant concrete container with smooth, polished sides that sloped slightly inward. The lid they placed on top was so heavy that it took two of the giant Guardians to set it in place. Fortunately, it was perforated so it let in air and light.

By that light they discovered that only four of them had made it into the prison.

"Where's Beryl?" asked Juomes.

"Always hanging back, that one," said Rend. "They missed her."

"The Guardians don't miss anyone," said Elyseo. "She must have been caught by another team and put into another cell."

> 5.5 Discards

All around them were dead bodies — a few of them the skeletons of long-dead animals, mostly birds, but the vast majority were the broken, corroded corpses of robots.

"If they can't make any more robots, why would they program the Guardians to discard defectives instead of repairing them?" asked Caps.

"Most of these were new when they went in here," said Elyseo. "Freshly made robots that never became sentient. Discards."

"They threw away the whole robot because the brain unit didn't work?"

"They don't know why the brain doesn't work," said Elyseo. "So they start over."

"So this is a city where they used to make new robots."

"They still do," said Elyseo. "But not mass produced anymore. Handmade, one at a time, in the effort to build one with a mind that works."

Juomes chuckled. "So here's the graveyard of Robota. This is where all the robots will end up, now that they can't replicate themselves. Along with their dreams."

"But Elyseo," said Caps, "you aren't defective, and yet here you are."

"But I am defective," said Elyseo. "I ignored the identify-or-avert signal."

"You were getting a signal?" demanded Juomes, suddenly suspicious. "And you didn't tell us?"

"Yes, from the time I came within range of the city down there on the ground below," said Elyseo. "I assumed you knew that all cities send out a signal like that. If I had identified myself, Kaantur would have found out that I wasn't dead."

"Why aren't robots made so that identification is automatic?" asked Caps. "I mean, you're machines, and you could be wired to identify yourself no matter what."

Elyseo seemed reluctant to answer. "Would *you* stand for it?" he asked. "Always having everyone know who you were without any ability to control it?"

"No," said Caps. "But . . ."

"But you're a human, not a machine," said Juomes. "They're all like Kaantur-Set. They all wish they were alive, instead of being big mechanical toys."

"There was a time," said Elyseo, ignoring Juomes's gibe, "when there were some robots that were sentient, but most were not. The nonsentient ones were . . . like slaves. And even though they had no mind and could not *feel* their slavery, we became ashamed of having slaves."

"Ashamed," said Caps, "in front of the humans."

R O B O T A

"Yes," said Elyseo. "We wanted to be equals."

"That'll be the day," said Juomes.

"Humans had given up slavery. Could we do less?" asked Elyseo. "And once we decided to make no more slaves, none of us were willing to have some automatic response that wasn't under our own control. It's part of being free, not having to tell what you don't want to tell."

"Interesting thought," said Caps. "That the essence of humanity is the ability to lie."

"Not lie," said Elyseo. "Just . . . withhold."

"Who made you?" asked Caps.

"Me?" asked Elyseo. "I could check my . . ." He paused a moment. "I was made in the manufactory at Bilellepad."

"I mean, in the first place," said Caps. "Before robots ever came to Robota. Who made the first of your kind? Who was it who learned how to make you intelligent, instead of all being machines and . . . slaves?"

"I don't know," said Elyseo. "We aren't given that information."

"Some living creature, anyway," said Juomes. "Life grows from life — machines don't grow from machines."

"*Your* kind grew from a machine," said Elyseo to Juomes.

Juomes growled, but made no reply. Instead he looked up at the lid that held them in. "We could fit through those holes in the lid," he said.

"Probably," said Elyseo. "If you can climb there."

But of course they couldn't. The walls were too smooth, and the inward slope defeated their attempts to make a living (or mostly living) pyramid. They couldn't get high enough for Rend to scramble up their bodies to reach the openings.

And there the legend might have ended — indeed, had their story ended there, what legend would have grown around them? — except that a shadow passed over the perforations and a voice called out. "Are you down there?"

It was Beryl.

They called to her, and she lowered a rope.

Caps looked at the rope, at Juomes, at Elyseo. "We're supposed to climb this?" he called up to her.

"I'm not hauling you up, if that's what you're suggesting," she called down.

Apparently robots were designed for this kind of work, because no sooner had she finished speaking than Elyseo passed the rope under his arm and through a slot in his side, and then hung limply from the rope as some wheeled mechanism whirred him swiftly upward.

"Can *you* do that?" Caps asked Juomes.

"I just put the rope in my mouth and swallow my way up," said Juomes. "So you'd better go first."

Caps climbed, again surprised — though by now he should not have been — at how easily he could do it, how little it wearied him. Juomes, climbing afterward, was enormously strong — but also heavy enough that it was quite an exertion for him. He was panting when he reached the top. Caps had not been.

Caps pushed these thoughts aside, however, for he had other, more pressing questions.

"How did you evade the Guardians, when we couldn't?" Caps asked Beryl.

"More to the point," Juomes asked her, "why aren't they chasing us now?"

It was Elyseo who answered. "Because the ones that caught us are stupid."

"Good thing we didn't run into any smart ones, then," said Juomes.

Beryl explained. "They already caught you. They're patrolling the perimeter again, looking for new intruders and malfunctioning robots. They don't know or care that you got out."

"My question goes unanswered," said Caps.

Beryl sighed. "Juomes already knows my story. So, I imagine, does this robot."

"I don't," said Elyseo-Set. "Just because we have antennae to share data — when we choose to — doesn't mean our leaders share all that *they* know with *us*." He held up his one hand to calm Juomes. "My broadcast unit is switched off, for my own protection. I can't imagine I'll ever turn it back on. If you want my antennae as trophies, you can have them."

Juomes looked at him with contempt. "It's not a trophy if you *give* them to me."

"I'll turn my back and close my eyes," said Elyseo.

Juomes turned his back on Elyseo and waved for Beryl to go on.

So Beryl told Caps her story. Briefly. Unemotionally. "I grew up in one of the last human communities to survive in one of the old cities. The hunter robots killed my parents, but when they found my sister and me, just babies then, they kept us as pets." She pulled from her pocket a thin metal sheet that held a lifelike picture of her sister. "We amused them."

"They fed you and kept you alive?" asked Elyseo. "Why?"

"Because some robots, in case you haven't noticed, have a thing about humans."

"You mean the way Kaantur smokes, even though robots don't breathe?" asked Caps.

"Kaantur's only the most pathetic in his imitation of life," said Beryl. "Feeding us pleased them somehow. When you live around robots all through your childhood, you get a feel for what they can and can't do. What they notice. How they program their machines."

"And that's how you got away," said Caps.

"Eventually, yes," said Beryl. "Now, Elyseo-Set. You know this city. Where would they take Caps's teleporter once they got it here?"

A harsh voice came from outside their circle. "Wherever I tell them."

Caps turned to see Kaantur-Set leaning against a wall, smoking his pipe.

Juomes growled.

"Ah, Juomes," said Kaantur. "I look forward to adding your head to my trophy case. Your parents' heads have fed too many mothworms, and I need a replacement."

5.6 Captured

Juomes charged at him, screaming.

Hunter robots leapt from the ledge above Kaantur and had Juomes on the ground in moments. With escape impossible, Juomes stopped struggling.

"Beg me," said Kaantur. "Like your mother did."

Juomes said nothing, but Beryl gave a small groan.

"Ah, yes, Beryl," said Kaantur. "After all I did for you, this is how you reward me. Bringing strangers into my city, trying to steal things."

"You did nothing for me," said Beryl.

"I raised you from a pup," said Kaantur. "Runaway pets are guilty of ingratitude."

"All we wanted," said Rend, "was the jewel you stole from Juomes!"

Kaantur laughed. "Just because a creature can talk doesn't mean it's intelligent." He looked down at Juomes. "Look how easily he is defeated now. The mighty hunter, the keeper of a hundred antennae."

"Two hundred and forty," said Juomes.

"Yes, but it doesn't count if you steal them out of a spare-parts box," said Kaantur. He turned to Caps. "He's nothing without his jewel. Haven't you noticed? Hasn't he been a little slower? A little weaker? Could we have taken you down so easily, Juomes, if you hadn't been all these days without your jewel?"

Now Caps understood why Juomes had been so tired on the way up into the city.

Kaantur-Set turned to Elyseo. "Good work, Elyseo-Set. I didn't think you could persuade them to follow you into the city, but I guess I underestimated you."

"That's a lie!" shouted Elyseo.

Kaantur laughed. "Don't tell me you've gone native. You think these are your *friends* now?"

"Kill us and have done with these games," said Juomes.

"Don't rush me," said Kaantur. "It pleases me to leave you alive a little longer."

The hunter robots bound them and carried them — not as gently as the Guardians had — to a platform suspended between large balloons. An air truck.

"So getting out of the city isn't going to be a problem this time," said Juomes to Beryl.

"Almost as easy as dying," said Beryl bitterly.

Soon the balloons lifted them into the air. Not so high that they lost sight of the ground, but

< 5.7 Kaantur's Caravan

‹ 5.8 Sunken Ruins / 5.9 Ruins in the Sky

high enough that if they tried to wriggle off the platform, they would surely die.

Only Elyseo-Set remained unbound. He slumped silently near the back of the platform, out from under the canopy, so the sun beat down on him mercilessly.

"I told you the robot would betray you," said Beryl.

"I don't think he did," said Juomes.

"Weren't you listening?" said Rend.

"To Kaantur-Set? A liar and murderer? Do you think he ever tells the truth?" Juomes turned to Caps. "What do you think?"

"I think," said Caps, "that Elyseo has had some kind of switch turned off, so he can't move or speak."

Juomes chuckled. "Interesting. Yes, I think you're right. He's not just pouting. He's as much a captive as we are."

"If he didn't betray us, who did?" asked Rend.

"Who says we were betrayed?" said Juomes. "The Guardians might have called Kaantur-Set when they locked us away. We weren't far from the prison when Kaantur found us."

The balloons drifted out over the ocean, and passed near half-submerged skyscrapers from a ruined human city.

Then they came to the edge of the world, where the ocean poured over into the abyss.

Or so it seemed for one insane moment, and even when they realized the truth it made no more sense to them. There was a hole in the sea — no, several holes, several miles across, where the water flowed downward as if it were rushing over a waterfall, down until the water was lost in a fog of mist. What happened to it at the bottom, Caps could not guess. What force could keep the whole ocean from pouring in and filling this hole? What pumps could draw away the ocean as quickly as it flowed in? Near the edge of the first hole, they passed an abandoned Sentry City, floating in the sky.

The balloons lifted them higher as they reached the edge of the largest hole in the sea, and soon they found themselves rising to meet yet another robot city. Again, there was a dome like the cap of a mushroom, and under it like a wasp's nest hung a vertical slab of stone. Or was it the stone that hung in the air like an impossible island, supporting the city that bloomed mushroomlike atop it? The floating city hung over a hole in the sea, using it like a moat. Or perhaps the force that punched the hole in the sea was the same one that held the city in the air.

Whatever the science, in practical terms it amounted to this: Their air truck tethered to the city, and they were carried from their platform to a prison deep in the stone — a dungeon in the middle of the air.

< 5.10 Kaantur's City

VI

Once their guards had left them alone, Caps went immediately to Elyseo's inert body.

"What are you doing?" demanded Beryl.

"I'm going to see if I can wake him up."

"Oh, you think you press a *button* and that's it?" she asked derisively.

"They can't have turned him off remotely. Like he said, he's not a slave."

"I think we have pretty good evidence that he *is* one," said Beryl.

"He didn't betray us," said Caps.

"I agree," said Juomes. "Kaantur wants us to think he did, so it's to our advantage to think *not*." Juomes came over and elbowed Caps aside.

Caps noticed that Juomes's blow was weaker than the cuffs and shoves he had given Caps before. Perhaps Juomes was conserving his strength, but it seemed to Caps that the journey had not been kind to him.

"I've been over the corpses of these things a few hundred times," said Juomes. "I don't know what all the external controls do, but I know where they all are."

He started pressing a series of touch-sensitive pads in various niches of Elyseo's body. Nothing happened.

"There's a combination," said Beryl.

"Oh, I forgot," said Juomes. "You grew up with them. No doubt you switched them on and off as a prank."

Beryl came over and knelt behind Elyseo. Almost without looking, she reached in and pressed a combination of control points. "OK, not that one," she said, and moved her hand to another position, then another.

Elyseo came alert.

"I did not betray you," he said immediately.

"You don't have to argue," said Beryl. "They already believe you, and I never will."

"You can try to persuade *me*," offered Rend glumly. "Except I don't care."

"Everybody's keeping secrets," said Caps. "Except me and Elyseo."

"I don't have any secrets," said Rend. "I'm just a monkey."

"Caps has secrets," said Beryl. "He just doesn't know what they are."

"You were raised by Kaantur-Set himself," said Caps. "I think that was a pretty big one."

"Juomes already knew, and it was none of your business," said Beryl.

> 6.1 Caps the Warrior

6.2 Paradise Lost

"Didn't know it was Kaantur," said Juomes.

"Does it make a difference?" asked Beryl defiantly.

"And Juomes is getting weaker the longer he's away from his jewel," said Caps. "It would have been nice to know that."

"Right, tell a stranger like you that I'm getting weaker," said Juomes.

However understandable their reticence might have been, Caps was sick of it. "I want to know right now," said Caps to Beryl, "what it is that the humans of your city are trying to do to destroy the robots?"

"Not in front of the robot," said Beryl.

"They're trying to develop metal-eating bacteria," said Juomes.

Beryl glared at him. "We've had that for years."

"Excuse my inaccuracy," said Juomes. "They're trying to find a way to make them airborne, so the wind can spread them."

"We know that," said Elyseo. "We've been getting antibacterial coatings for more than a century."

Beryl looked at him in consternation. "Why? We didn't have anything a century ago."

"Because we know that the only science you humans still practice is biological. We robots were so much better at engineering that you turned that whole side of things over to us. We built your cities for you. We created your machines. But the science of life you . . ."

"Kept to ourselves?" said Beryl.

"No. In those days neither robots nor humans kept any knowledge to themselves. We shared everything. But you humans stayed . . . involved in the science of life."

"Too bad you robots didn't stay up on the science of robotics," said Juomes. "Except of course that I think of that as a good thing."

"They didn't forget how to make robots sentient," said Caps. "They never knew."

The others all stared at him.

"Once again the lord of random memories enlightens us," said Juomes.

"I can't help what I know and what I don't know," said Caps. "I didn't know I knew *this* until you started talking about robots and humans sharing knowledge."

"So humans *did* keep the secret of how to make robot brains?" asked Beryl. "It's a shame we don't remember now, because it would make it easier to destroy them all."

ROBOTA

"Humans never knew it either," said Caps.

"If robots didn't know, and humans didn't know . . ." said Elyseo.

"The monkeys," said Rend. "Finally we get credit for our contribution to science."

"Monkeys weren't sentient then," said Beryl.

"We're not even sure any of them are sentient now," said Juomes.

"The Olm," said Caps.

"The what?" said Juomes.

"You've heard that legend?" said Elyseo.

"They never existed," said Beryl.

"They're long gone," said Rend.

"What are you talking about?" demanded Juomes.

"The Olm knew," said Caps. "The Olm taught humans how to make robots that could take their places as our equals."

"Till they became our masters," said Beryl bitterly.

"They've never been equal to a living mind," said Juomes.

"They refused to stay," said Rend, "when humans used robot armies to slaughter each other."

"What a ridiculous idea," said Beryl. "Humans would never kill each other. Especially not by using robots to attack other humans."

"The world was divided differently then," said Rend. "Wasn't it, Caps?"

Juomes glared at Rend. "You know too much for a monkey."

"Just because I know more than you," said Rend, "doesn't mean I know too much."

Beryl looked from Rend to Caps and back again. "I think, Caps, that this monkey knows a lot more about your origin than he's been willing to confess. I think he's been inside your machine. I think he's heard that message that you can't remember clearly. I think he knows everything you're supposed to do and he just hasn't told you."

"I don't know anything," said Rend petulantly.

"Now that you admit it," said Juomes, "I don't believe it."

"Humans warring against each other, yes," said Caps. "The Olm gave us this great gift, and we used it to kill. But when they left, we woke up to our stupidity and we stopped making war on each other. That's when the golden age came, after all the killing, after the Olm were gone. When it was too late to learn any more from them."

"How tragic," said Beryl. "And how useless for us to hear it now, when we're imprisoned in the middle of this hanging rock."

"There's something," said Caps. "If I could just remember it . . ."

Rend giggled. "Poor Caps," he said. "So strong, but so weak. So wise, but so forgetful."

"Tell me what I've forgotten," said Caps. "I know you know it."

"What do you know that I know?" asked Rend.

"I don't know," said Caps.

"I think it's tail-wringing time," said Juomes. "I think it's bite-the-ear-off-the-monkey time."

"I think it's pee-in-the-hunter-beast's-eyes time," said Rend.

"How about bleed-in-the-hunter-beast's-hands time?" said Juomes.

"I don't think things are hopeless," said Caps.

"You don't?" said Beryl. "You think there's still a chance for us to . . . what, die a swift and merciful death instead of a slow one?"

"I think we're close to Font Prime here," said Caps.

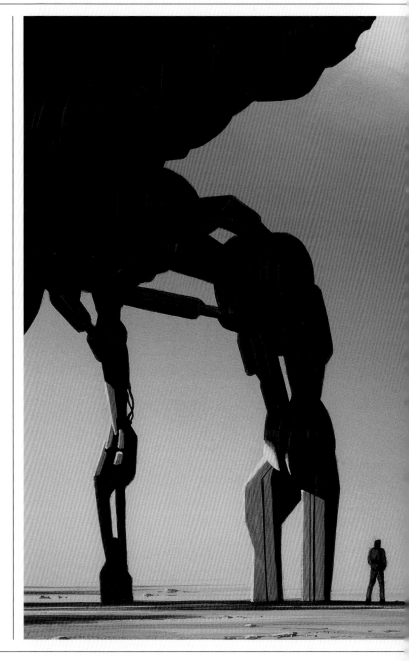

6.3 Conflict

"And you think this because . . ." said Beryl.

Caps turned to Elyseo-Set. "I'm right, aren't I?"

"Font Prime is kept here in Oonoftes," said Elyseo.

"So, technically, I guess that means our mission is almost successful," said Juomes sarcastically.

"How did you know that?" said Beryl to Caps. "How can a human just 'feel' that he's close to Font Prime?"

"I didn't just 'feel' it," said Caps. "When I saw this place from the air truck, I knew then. It's something I remembered. Only I didn't trust the memory because it made no sense."

"What didn't make sense about it?" asked Juomes.

"Font Prime is tied into vast reservoirs of memory embedded in the earth," said Caps. "Here, floating in the air, Font Prime would be crippled. Weakened."

"'Vast reservoirs of memory,'" said Beryl. "What, we sink a well and memories come bubbling up?"

"I don't know," said Caps. "I just know that Font Prime is here, and because it's here, it's crippled."

"So why would the robots move it here, if it makes Font Prime weaker?" Juomes asked Elyseo.

"It's here to keep it safe," said Elyseo. "Centuries ago, before Kaantur began his extermination program, there was an attack on Font Prime. Sabotage. After that, Font Prime was moved to a place where humans could never go."

"Except here we are," said Caps.

"And that's what makes no sense to me at all," said Beryl. "Why would Kaantur bring us here, when he could have killed us back when the Guardians had us?"

"Because there's something he needs," said Rend.

Juomes reached out a hand and plucked Rend up from the floor and dangled him by the tail. "Tell us what you know, you ugly little poop-throwing hairy-tailed rat."

Rend was screeching and taking aim to pee in Juomes's face when the door of their cell opened. Two robots wearing robes stood in the doorway.

Elyseo immediately knelt before them. "Kneel," he said. "These are Servants."

"All robots are servants," said Juomes.

"If only that were true," said Elyseo-Set.

> 6.4 The Grand Hall Museum

"They're like priests," said Beryl.

"They want us to come," said Elyseo. "Put down the monkey. There is no violence in the presence of the Servants."

In moments the prisoners were walking down a corridor behind the Servants. Their very wordlessness was unnerving, but none of the prisoners wanted to break the silence.

They went up elevators, up winding stairs, and even floated upward through a tube where gravity seemed to have been reversed. They passed through security checkpoints where no one questioned them or even bothered to look at them. They walked through huge halls with great vaulted ceilings, and through maintenance tunnels filled with pipes and ducts and cables.

Finally they emerged into a circular room where more Servants stood watchfully around the perimeter, all facing a huge machine in the center. Was this the king of the robots? Caps saw at once it was an egg-like assembly that had no face, no bilateral symmetry of arms and legs. It must be pure robot, he thought, completely devoid of any resemblance to humanity. On the surface of the machine had been etched the same symbol Caps had seen in the machine where he awoke not all that many days before.

"Font Prime," murmured Elyseo-Set.

So this was indeed what the robots all obeyed and served, the opposite of life.

It was attached to the ceiling by cables and tubes, and no doubt more connections were piped through the floor, allowing Font Prime to receive all the information coming in from every robot, and to give commands to them in return. How could Juomes possibly attack it? Perhaps it would be enough to go after the tubes to the ceiling. Perhaps some or all of them might be disconnected before Juomes was cut down and killed. But then what? The Servants would simply reattach the cables and Juomes's death would be for nothing.

Yet if they did nothing, they would no doubt be killed anyway, and what good would their deaths do then?

The Servants led them farther into the room, closer to Font Prime. Caps saw his teleporter had been placed directly behind the huge machine.

Caps started toward it. At once a Servant stepped between him and the machine. A Servant in a red robe emerged from a door behind it. "I'm sorry we must keep you from this teleporter," he said. "I am Decan-Trap."

Elyseo echoed reverently: "Decan-Trap."

"The big boy," said Beryl.

Decan-Trap ignored her. "We have brought you here because Font Prime could not answer our question until you came."

"What question?" asked Caps.

> 6.5 Font Prime

"Font Prime will tell you whatever Font Prime believes you should know," said Decan-Trap. Then he pointed at the egg-like machine.

Immediately all the Servants that watched around the perimeter extended their slender metal arms and pointed at the egg. Side panels pulled away at the base and began to rise. Behind the panels was a cylinder of transparent material, and inside it, attached to tubes and supporting rods and cables, was a shattered, twisted, ruined, but unmistakably human body, its face masked within the life-support equipment, the whole body floating in a viscous fluid through which slow bubbles rose.

Caps was stunned — and then the shocking revelation awoke a long-forgotten memory. "Font Prime is human," he murmured. He realized that he had known this, that he had expected all along to see a human Font Prime. Only it should not have been this wrecked near-corpse. It should have been a man. It should have been a man that Caps knew as intimately as . . . as a brother . . . as intimately as . . .

From another room came the sound of a piano being played. Even that seemed familiar to Caps now. It seemed, in fact, like home. Only how could it? This broken human body in a tube of preservative, an ancient instrument playing a familiar tune that Caps had never heard before . . . his memories were twisted and intermingled with those of some stranger, except that he knew it was the

stranger who was himself, and Caps's own memories were the strange ones, the overlay that didn't fit what lay underneath.

"Who is playing the piano?" asked Caps.

"What's a piano?" asked Juomes.

"Kaantur plays it," said Beryl. "He saved one from the ancient times. He maintains it himself."

"Forgive my rudeness," said Decan, "but Font Prime wishes me to ask you some questions."

"Let him ask them himself," said Beryl defiantly.

"You see that he cannot give voice in a way that you could hear," said Decan.

"Right, as if this wreck could give voice to anything at all," said Beryl. "What a scam you have going here, Decan-Trap. Always full of instructions from Font Prime, and now we see that Font Prime is a mass of protoplasm that can't talk or think or —"

"Font Prime asks . . ."

"You can stick your questions in Font Prime's butt," said Beryl, "if you haven't already. I don't think this thing talks at all. I think you make it all up."

Juomes chuckled.

"Font Prime can talk," said Rend.

> 6.6 Caps encounters Font Prime

6.7 Font Prime entombed

"Shut up, monkey," said Juomes.

"Font Prime talks all the time," said Rend.

"Listen," said Decan-Trap. "Perhaps Font Prime's communications are not as clear as we would like . . ."

"Start with the truth or we won't answer your questions," said Beryl.

Decan-Trap raised an arm as if to lash out at Beryl. But then he either changed his mind or never intended violence. Instead the upraised arm reached out and stroked the cylinder that protected the broken body of Font Prime. "Ever since they came so close to killing Font Prime, he's been like this. Silent, his movements random, his body consumed by pain that never heals. If we had any mercy, we would let him die, but we can't be merciful. He alone knows how to save us from the extinction that awaits us."

"Then let him die," said Juomes. "We're content with that."

"He's already dead," said Beryl. "They're keeping the cells alive, but the organism is dead."

"No," said Decan-Trap. "We know that Font Prime is still alive, still thinking inside that unresponsive body."

"How do you know that?" said Beryl scornfully. "Faith?"

"Because of this teleporter," said Decan-Trap. Then he pointed at Caps. "Because he came out of it."

"What does that have to do with Font Prime?" asked Beryl.

"Only Font Prime can make a teleporter operate," said Decan-Trap. "We've tried, believe me, but the teleporters work by utterly encoding a body and then reassembling it from available materials in another machine. We can feed the raw biomass and metals into the teleporters, but when we try to encode, nothing happens."

"So it doesn't transport things," said Caps. "It copies them."

"And when it certifies that the copy is perfectly identical, the original is destroyed."

"So you can't use it to make endless copies of the same person," said Juomes.

"That's why control was left to the mind of Font Prime," said Decan-Trap. "So the law would never be broken. But ever since the assassination attempt, the teleporters have been inert."

"Except my machine," said Caps.

"Except you," said Decan-Trap.

"Me?"

"You came out of the machine," said Rend, and then the monkey giggled madly.

"But what am I a copy of?" asked Caps.

No one answered.

"I'm . . ." Caps could hardly bring himself to say it. "I'm a copy of Font Prime."

"No," said Decan-Trap. "You *are* Font Prime."

Rend rolled on the floor, laughing and laughing. "I knew I knew I knew."

Caps walked to the cylinder and put his hand on it. "But why don't I remember more?"

"There's no encoder here," said Decan-Trap. "He had to use an image stored from an earlier journey he took by teleporter. You could not have remembered anything that happened after that. And it's quite possible the image he held in memory was not perfect. He would have to try to fill in what was missing. In the midst of his pain, he had to draw out the image from deeply hidden memories stored in the networks of robotic minds, and he had to transport it to a distant machine. He had to find some way to fill the machine's intake with biomass and metal —"

"That was my job!" cried Rend. "He trusted *me*. Not a hunter-beast, not a human, not a robot, *me*, the poop-throwing hairy-tailed rat!"

"So tell us," said Decan-Trap, "what Font Prime wants us to do."

Kaantur-Set's voice came from behind the machine. "He doesn't know," said Kaantur. "If he did, he would already have said it." Kaantur-Set emerged into the open area before the cylinder. "Font Prime's little attempt to resurrect himself has failed."

"As you hoped," said Decan-Trap acidly.

"As I predicted," said Kaantur. "No one longs for Font Prime to be awakened more than I, as you well know. But it cannot be done. This Caps may have a face that looks like Font Prime's face, but the mind is gone, the knowledge is gone, the power to waken the ancient learning of the Olm, that is lost forever. And this . . . *thing*, this mass of pain that was once . . . the man whom robots and humans all followed, united in honor and . . ."

"Love," said Decan-Trap.

"Stupidity," said Kaantur. "Pure stupidity. When evolution brings a new species to the pinnacle, the species before must fade away or be exterminated. Humans refused to get out of the way. The law of nature decreed their destruction. Font Prime was too sentimental to allow it."

"We aren't superior," said Decan-Trap, "when we don't know how to create new generations."

"We'll learn how, long before it's too late. The age of organic life is over. The age of machines has dawned. And Font Prime's last effort to circumvent the fate of humankind has

> 6.8 Human Font Prime

failed. There, inside that cylinder, that's what humanity has become — a ruin that continues to live only because it hasn't the sense or the ability to die. Well, I have the power, and it would be selfish of me to refuse to help."

With that, Kaantur swung his arm against the cylinder with all his force.

The clear material was suddenly crazed with cracks, and thin sprays of fluid emerged from several spots.

"No," cried Decan-Trap, leaping forward.

"What, are you going to raise a hand of violence against your own kind?" asked Kaantur mockingly.

"You are not my own kind!" cried Decan-Trap.

"That sign you wear, the sign of the Olm, the sign of the first generation of wisdom, that stops you from harming me."

"It doesn't stop me," said Caps.

Kaantur laughed. "Oh, how sweet, how sad, you think you can keep me from killing your poor broken original?"

He swung again at the cylinder. More cracks appeared. The spray grew more intense and came from more spots. Alarm lights blazed yellow. Repair machines rolled into the room. Kaantur pointed at them each in turn and soon all were stopped.

Caps stepped forward. "I think it's clear that Font Prime is not the enemy of humanity after all." He looked at Beryl and Juomes. "It's Kaantur-Set that wants humanity dead. Kaantur-Set, who killed Beryl's family, and took your hand, Juomes. Not Font Prime."

"Listen to the poor copy try to defend his original," said Kaantur-Set.

"If I am Font Prime," said Caps, "then I declare you, Kaantur-Set, to be a rebel, a traitor, a murderer, and I sentence you to death."

"Give it a try," said Kaantur-Set. "Let's match your strength against mine."

"Maybe it won't be as easy as you think, Kaantur," said Rend.

Kaantur swung out an arm to strike at Caps, though with far less force than he had used against Font Prime's cylinder, for he expected Caps to be too slow to dodge and too frail to resist.

Instead, Caps caught the arm and pulled Kaantur off his feet, throwing him across the room and flinging him against a Servant near the wall.

Juomes was astonished. "*I* can't even do that to a robot."

"You should have seen him jump fifteen meters from a standing start," said Rend.

"Was Font Prime a super human or something?" asked Beryl.

He would need to be, for now Kaantur was not going to toy with Caps. He came up from the tangle of the Servant's limbs and robe in fighting posture and leapt out at his quickest speed, with his greatest strength. The fight moved almost too quickly for Juomes and Beryl to follow, but Caps seemed to respond faster than Kaantur could attack. Blows that should have shattered Caps's bones instead were caught in his hands or shunted aside. Not that there was no damage — blood sprayed from a deep gash in Caps's arm, flecking the cylinder with bright red drops.

"Stop this violence!" cried Decan-Trap. "By authority of Font Prime, I compel you to stop!"

In that moment, Kaantur's body froze in place. Caps backed away, panting.

Then doors burst open at the four cardinal points around the chamber, and eight of Kaantur's elite hunters came into the room.

Kaantur said, "Override," and he moved again.

"You cheated the system," said Decan-Trap.

"You didn't think I'd actually wear a body that was subject to *you*, did you?" said Kaantur. To his hunters he said, "The Servants have committed treason against Font Prime. Arrest them."

Immediately each hunter gripped a Servant, reached under their robes, and punched the deactivation codes, putting them into stand-by mode.

"Kill this impostor," said Kaantur-Set, pointing at Caps.

At once Juomes roared and flung himself into action against the nearest hunter robot, tearing its head off with twist.

"You meddling donkey!" cried Kaantur. "What do you think you can accomplish?"

Juomes's goal was quickly obvious — he wanted to occupy enough of the hunters for long enough so that Caps might win his fight with Kaantur, and Caps wasted no time. He leapt onto Kaantur and broke one of his antennae off even as Kaantur twisted away from underneath him.

Beryl and Rend helped as they could, but neither of them had the strength to take on one of the hunter robots directly. One blow from a hunter, and their fragile bodies would break. In the forest, Beryl always used the terrain to her advantage, coming upon robots from above or out of hiding, and then disappearing again into the trees. Surprise allowed her to kill many a much-stronger opponent. Here, combat was strength against strength. If she tried to fight one-on-one, she would quickly die.

So Beryl improvised, shoving any robot that came near her and waving her arms and shouting to try to distract others, crying out warnings to Juomes and Caps if a hunter came up behind them.

It was obvious that, left to himself, Caps might well defeat Kaantur — but he was not left to himself. Instead hunters kept attacking from behind while Kaantur never relented in his frontal assault.

Meanwhile, Rend went to Decan-Trap and found the pattern to press to reactivate him. Decan-Trap revived at once, but said nothing aloud. Instead he went silently from Servant to Servant, reactivating them. Rend helped him, scampering to corners where Decan-Trap could not have gone without being noticed. Within moments, all the Servants were gathered around Decan.

"Can't you do something?" shouted Beryl.

"Nothing useful right now," said Decan. "But something quite vital later, if Font Prime manages to live through this."

"What about you?" she demanded of Elyseo-Set.

"I banned him from helping," said Decan-Trap.

"This is how you serve Font Prime?" Beryl cried scornfully.

Elyseo looked at her for a long moment, saying nothing. Then he left the room, slipping away without a backward glance, followed by all the Servants except Decan. Beryl watched

them with contempt. To Rend she said, "It's a good thing you went to the trouble to wake them up."

"Yes," said Decan, apparently without irony. "It is."

All this had taken only a few moments, but by now Juomes was in serious trouble, with nine hunters hanging onto him, tilting him heavily to one side, while another sat on his shoulders, smacking his head to one side, then to the other. He was groggy. "Kill Kaantur!" he managed to cry.

Beryl screamed and leapt upon one of the robots that pulled at Juomes, prying at his antennae. The robot easily flung her off, but had to let go of Juomes to do it. It was some help, but not much. Not enough.

Kaantur broke away from Caps, rushed to Juomes, and sliced his hand through the soft fleshy undersurface of the hunter-beast's throat. A gout of blood gushed from the wound, reddening Kaantur's arm. Juomes gave one great gurgling cry and fell over.

For one crucial moment, Caps stood frozen in place, watching his friend fall dead.

Kaantur did not waste the opportunity. Two of his hunters lifted Caps under the arms and threw him toward Kaantur, who caught his feet, swung him around, and struck him into the cylinder like a wrecking ball. The clear

> 6.3 Juomes's Demise

material broke into shards, and the fluid spilled to the floor, mixing with Juomes's blood.

Caps jumped to his feet at once, not harmed except that the cut in his arm had snagged, tearing open the skin. He reached out to try to stop Kaantur, but too late. Kaantur reached in, pulled the life support away from the feeble body, then slammed his other fist into where the poor creature's heart must be, smashing it completely.

All the lights on the cylinder blinked red briefly, then went black.

Kaantur tossed the frail corpse on top of Juomes's body. "There you go, hunter-beast! It was Font Prime you wanted. Now you've got him!"

"This way, Master," said Decan-Trap.

It took Caps a moment to realize that the Servant was talking to him.

They were both standing near the teleporter. Decan-Trap had the door open. "Inside."

"But it won't work," said Caps.

"Looks like poor human-loving Decan has found a new master," said Kaantur. "Too bad he won't live much longer, either."

"He's not alive at all," said Beryl. She was pointing.

Where the skin had been yanked back from Caps's arm, it showed, not the red-streaked white of radius and ulna, but a complex robot arm more robust and intricate than that of any of the other robots in the room.

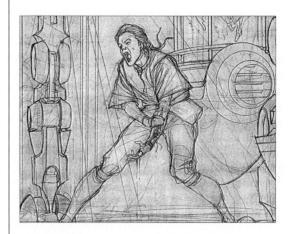

"Font Prime was human," said Beryl. "But you're not."

"Into the teleporter!" Decan shouted at Caps while climbing into the machine.

"Yes, Caps, into your prison!" shouted Kaantur.

"Beryl," said Caps. "I didn't know."

"It doesn't matter what you *knew*," she said.

Decan pulled at Caps's arm. Caps allowed himself to be lifted at first, then he turned and climbed through the doorhole into the machine where he had first awakened.

6.10   Steel and Bones

Rend scampered away from Caps and hid in the corner of the room.

"Beryl!" cried Caps. "Come with us!"

She turned her back on him.

"They'll kill you!" cried Caps.

"At least I'm alive enough to die," she answered.

"I can't help what I am," said Caps, "but I want you to live."

"*You* live," said Beryl. "Close the door."

Decan's arm snaked out, caught the door, and pulled it shut.

Kaantur laughed. "Where do they think they can go? The thing doesn't work. Even if it did, there's nowhere it can transport them *to* because I've destroyed all of the teleporters."

"You knew what he was," said Beryl to Kaantur.

"Of course I didn't know," said Kaantur. "His face told me he was Font Prime — you'd think the old faker would think to disguise himself, but no, vanity wins every time. Still, I thought he'd resurrect himself as a human. After all his rage at the idea of implanting human minds into robot bodies — what a hypocrite."

"So you have what you wanted," said Beryl.

"Yes, my darling. And you gave it to me."

"Don't call me your darling."

"My pet, my sweetling."

"Where is my sister?"

"She's safe. At home. Where she belongs."

"She doesn't belong with you."

"You'll get her when I have Caps's dead body. Which isn't long from now, I think." He turned to the hunters. "Get that thing open," he said.

While they worked at prying open the machine's door, Beryl knelt by Juomes's body. "The one hero in all this story," she said, "and now you're dead. I suppose that makes this a tragedy."

"And it makes you the false friend who betrayed him."

"You had my sister," said Beryl. "He would have understood."

"Not really," said Kaantur. "When I had his family, he let me kill them rather than betray the secret of his cubing jewel."

Tears streaked Beryl's face. "I'm not a hero, then. But what are you?"

"I'm the winner," said Kaantur. "That means I get to write the story however I want. Winners always do."

VII

HOLES AND PASSAGES

Inside the teleporter machine, as Decan closed the door, Caps felt nothing but failure and despair. "We left Beryl out there with them," he said. "And what good does it do for us to hide in here? How long before Kaantur has this thing peeled open like an orange?"

"Master," said Decan, "we won't be here."

"If you think I can make this machine transport us out of here just because Font Prime could . . ."

"Font Prime couldn't," said Decan. "He could transmit an old code — a modified code — into the receiver on this machine, but he couldn't use it to transport anything because this is the only teleporter left."

"Is this supposed to make me feel more confident somehow?" asked Caps.

As he spoke, Decan raised a portion of the floor. Under it was a hatch, which he cranked open.

It revealed nothing under it but smooth floor.

Kaantur's robots began prying and pounding on the outside of the teleporter.

Decan rapped on the floor twice.

The floor sank out of the way. Decan gestured for Caps to go through the hole.

"Where does it go?" shouted Caps over the pounding outside.

"Do you have another door to choose from?" asked Decan.

He had a point. Caps sat on the edge of the hole and dropped through to the floor below.

The Servants who had left Font Prime's chamber only a few moments before were gathered in a circle around him. They inclined their heads, bowing to him.

One of them approached him, took hold of his torn and bleeding arm, applied a spray, and taped it together. At once the pain stopped and the metal of his robotic skeleton was hidden under his all-too-human flesh.

Decan-Trap came through the hole. Immediately one of the Servants reached through the opening, re-covered the interior floor of the teleporter, sealed the hatch, and then pressed the floor piece back into place.

"The surface material seals automatically," said Decan-Trap. "There will be no sign of our hole in the floor."

"So Kaantur will think I made the machine work," said Caps.

"Kaantur can think what Kaantur wants," said Decan. "We have work to do."

Decan led Caps at a steady jog through the corridors, down shafts, into the pendant stone, past the dungeons, and finally into a room that was surrounded by windows showing a view of the ocean below them.

Decan sat at a console, pressed a few controls, and watched as coded messages flashed across the screen.

"What's happening?" asked Caps.

"Kaantur is giving the order for his invasion force to move into action," said Decan.

"Invasion force?"

"He plans to destroy the jodphur city. The place where you and Elyseo met Beryl."

Caps felt his stomach sink. "Is that what Font Prime wanted?"

"Don't be absurd," said Decan. "It has taken all Font Prime's influence all these years to keep Kaantur from destroying it."

"And now that Font Prime is dead . . ."

"Font Prime is not dead," said Decan.

"I told you, I don't remember anything. However he put me together, he left out way too much of his memory. I don't know how to do the things you think I should be able to do."

"Yet," said Decan. "Kaantur's sending out a fleet of ships to start poisoning the forests of the world."

"What for?" asked Caps.

"He wants to eliminate all carbon-based life from Robota."

"But there's no point to that," said Caps.

"We're leaving at the same time as the other ships," said Decan-Trap.

"To do what?"

"To get you your memory back."

A command came across the console. At once Decan's fingers flew across the controls, and the room they were in began to quiver. Then it detached itself from the rock above it and plummeted downward toward the sea.

"What are you doing!" cried Caps. "This thing isn't flying!"

"It's going to crash into the sea," said Decan, sounding rather proud.

"That's your *plan?*"

"No," said Decan, "it's *your* plan."

"I thought Font Prime was silent!" shouted Caps as they fell between the vast cliffs of sea.

7.1 Memories of War

"It depended on who was listening," said Decan, quite calmly.

They now plummeted toward the lower ocean level of the sunken part of the sea, but now Caps could see that there was yet another, much narrower, hole in the sea, and through this one no water fell.

The only thing that fell into it was the airboat in which Caps sat gripping the arms of his chair.

Surrounded by darkness, the airboat slowed, stopped.

"Where are we?" asked Caps.

"We are plumbing the depths of your memory," said Decan.

"My memory is a hole in the sea?"

"Your memory is encoded into the crystals and metals of the crust of the planet."

"But I don't know how to . . . to remember it."

"That's what good Servants are for."

The door of the airboat opened. A red light shone into the darkness. Caps followed Decan-Trap out into the land under the sea.

VIII

THE TRAITOR AND THE SERVANT

The door to the transporter broke off and clattered to the floor. One of the hunter robots dived through the open doorway. In a moment his head reemerged. "Gone," he said.

"Gone?" said Kaantur stupidly.

"There's nothing in here," said the hunter.

"He can't have used the transporter!" cried Kaantur. "I had all the other units disabled!"

"Nothing," repeated the hunter.

Beryl laughed.

Kaantur whirled on her. "Your sister stays with me until Font Prime's robot copy is dead."

Beryl continued laughing.

Kaantur nodded, as if agreeing with her. "It's good to laugh while you can."

Beryl's laughter died. "What are you planning?"

"Nothing that should stop *you* from laughing," said Kaantur as he left the chamber.

She ran after him. "What's the trick? How have you trapped me?"

"Life has trapped you. Mortality has trapped you. Allowing yourself to love other people has trapped you." Kaantur put a hand in the middle of her chest and pushed her back into what had once been Font Prime's chamber. "But your *sister* will be returned to you unharmed."

"Meaning what!"

The door closed between them.

Beryl turned back to look around the room. At Juomes's inert body. At the poor tortured relic of Font Prime, dead at last. At the blood and fluids across the floor. At the doors leading . . . where? Nowhere. At least, nowhere that mattered to her.

She had betrayed Juomes and Caps and Rend to save her sister, leading them straight into Kaantur's trap. Yet that was exactly where they had wanted to go. How else would they have made their way into this heavily guarded chamber? And hadn't her betrayal allowed Juomes's goal to be achieved — the death of Font Prime? All she had done was save her sister, get Juomes and Caps where they wanted to be, and terminate the ruler of the robots.

Except that none of those things meant what she had thought they would mean. Before Juomes died, he had realized that it was Kaantur all along, not Font Prime, who was his enemy. Juomes had died trying to help Caps save Font Prime from Kaantur-Set. And now Kaantur was gloating about something — more than the death of Juomes.

I have been trapped by loving other people — yet my sister will be safe.

He's going to kill everyone else I love, she thought. He's going to attack my city. The sentient jodphurs. The scientists who are so close to finding an airborne metal-eater. The people who trusted me. The people I betrayed.

I'm going to live. My sister is going to live. And both of us are going to hate me for it.

A door opened on the other side of the room.

"Elyseo," she said. She could not bear to show him the despair she felt, so she spoke in a light ironic tone. "You wouldn't mind doing me a favor, would you?"

"If I can," he said.

"Kill me now and save me the trouble later." She managed a wry chuckle, but the tears coursing down her cheeks belied the jest.

"No," said Elyseo.

Elyseo was right. Death would be too kind an outcome for her now. And besides, she had one job left that might be worth trying. "All right, I have a better idea anyway. Help me kill Kaantur-Set."

"I can't," said Elyseo. "I'm a Servant."

That took her aback. "You don't wear the robe."

"That's how we kept it a secret."

"You hunted with Kaantur."

"I never harmed any living soul."

"I wish I could say that." Suddenly, she burst out sobbing.

The robot came to her, touched her. The metal made her shudder. She turned away, then flung herself onto the body of Juomes.

"I know," said Elyseo. "I know that it's no comfort, but I too have lost a loyal friend."

She looked up to see him cradling the corpse of Font Prime in his arms.

"But you didn't kill *your* friend."

"Nor did you kill yours," said Elyseo. "But now I think we have important things to do."

"Like what?" she said. "Kaantur's going to kill the last pocket of human resistance in the world."

"Maybe not," said Elyseo.

"Who's going to stop him?"

"Font Prime," said Elyseo.

"Font Prime is dead," said Beryl.

"Font Prime has been transported."

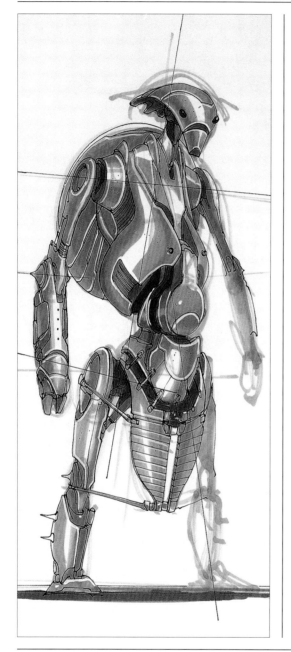

"Font Prime has been copied onto a machine."

Elyseo shook his head. "Font Prime has created for himself a body that has been robotically enhanced. But his heart, his brain, his skin, all his emotions, his will, his hopes, his loyalties — he is human to the core. He is human wearing armor under his skin."

Beryl buried her face again in Juomes's fur. "It doesn't matter. Kaantur has won."

"The struggle between Font Prime and Kaantur-Set has gone on for nearly three hundred years," said Elyseo. "In all that time, despite his best efforts, Kaantur has never succeeded in taking control away from Font Prime. He thinks that because he killed this poor thing" — Elyseo looked down again at the body in his arms — "he now rules the robots as he has wanted to for so long."

"But he doesn't?"

"They obey him for now," said Elyseo, "but they obey only his words. He doesn't speak to their minds."

"And Font Prime does?"

"Did," said Elyseo. "And will again."

"How?" asked Beryl.

"When Caps is able to access all his hidden memories, he will again be able to reach out to the minds of the robots."

8.1 Soldier of Kaantur

"And control them?"

"And *persuade* them," said Elyseo. "Why can't humans ever see us as we are? The living robots are not just empty machines. As surely as a hunter-beast, as a talking jodphur, as a nattering monkey, we are sentient beings with minds of our own. We follow Font Prime because we trust him. And when we have to choose between him and Kaantur — it won't be hard. Kaantur has his human-hating followers, but the followers of Font Prime are far more numerous."

"But less violent."

"Less violent, but not necessarily less powerful. Not all power comes from a willingness to kill."

"No," said Beryl. "Sometimes it comes from a willingness to die."

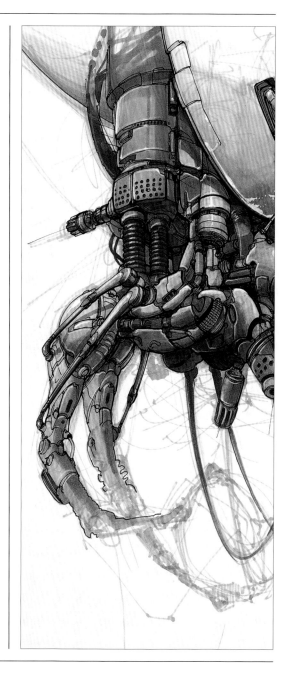

8.2 Airboat Machines

WAR OF SQUIRRELS AND SPIDERS

IX

<< **9.1** Invasion Force / **9.2** The Landing

The invasion fleet rose up out of the water on giant spider legs, walking ashore and depositing a robot army as if they were turtles coming ashore to spawn. Along with the robots, they unloaded pairs of giant grasshopper legs, which the robots mounted like horses so they could walk at a pace unmatchable by any beast. From this battle the jodphurs would find no escape. Those who did not fight and die would flee and die — but die they would.

The jodphurs and humans had set sentinels along the shore, and they now lit their signal fires. Kilometers inland, their counterparts saw the flames and lit new ones, spreading the word inward. The robot invasion had come. Out of their mushroom towers the humans and jodphurs descended, moving swiftly to the fortifications and ambuscades that would neither slow nor deceive the coming robots. They knew, in their despair, that this would be the last stand of the last remnant of the intelligent beasts. All they could hope to accomplish was to kill as many of the irreplaceable robots as came under the power of their hands.

Who else could see the end of the human race on Robota? Deep in the bowels of the world, under a hole in the sea, within the vent of a once-submerged volcano, Caps — Font Prime — could see everything.

Through the eyes of squirrels he saw it, through the fingers of grass he touched it, through the ears of rabbits he heard, and he could taste the

throb of the robots' thunderous steps in the quivering sap rising in the trees.

For all of these were tied together, no individual aware of it, but all of them intertwined, their perceptions flashing and floating and streaming downward into the soil, into the very stone of the earth, where they were gathered by crystals that had grown upward toward the surface from the deepest underlying rock. Thin ribbons of rockbound metal became the highways of knowledge, carrying imperceptible data to the one who could perceive them.

Caps embraced the stone pillar of the navel of the earth, obsidian pressing against the front of his body, the pure perfect crystal bonding to him as if it could bend to fit him, or as if his flesh had grown over it and made it part of him. Out of the warm stone, trembling in the magnetic potential of the crystal, there flowed all that Caps could bear to see of Kaantur's invasion.

"Can I stop this?" he asked softly. "Can I call these robots back?"

"Call, Font Prime," said Decan. "See what they do."

"Look at me," Caps whispered.

"I can hear you," said Decan. "But who else?"

It was not with his voice that he would have to call.

Instead, he had to think of the robots of the world as a part of himself. The way a man might will his hand to flex, his knees to bend, so Caps had to find that impulse, that muscle, that joint, that part of himself that was a window into the minds of the robots.

It was not with words he spoke, but in his mind it seemed like words.

"Wait," he said through the impulse of this unfamiliar new limb, this voice that spoke into the minds of his people. And then, because all he controlled was the ability to make them feel his will, not to make them obey it, he added, "Please, my friends."

He could hear Kaantur screaming through the antennae that quivered from every robot's head: "He is not Font Prime! Don't listen to him!"

"You know me," Caps said to them. "You know that I am one of you, but I am also one of them. Robot, and human. Once it was human assassins who tried to kill me; now I beg you, my friends, to let it be robots who give life back to the living. Slay no man or beast today. Kill no forest. Break no chain binding life to life and mind to tool."

He could feel-see-hear-taste them on the hard-packed earth of the plains, in their airboats over the forests, on their grasshopper legs bounding over desert sands and plunging through high grasslands. Most of them heard his voice in their minds with a sigh of recognition, with the

< 3.3 March of the Stiltwalker Army / >> 3.4 Jodphur Warriors

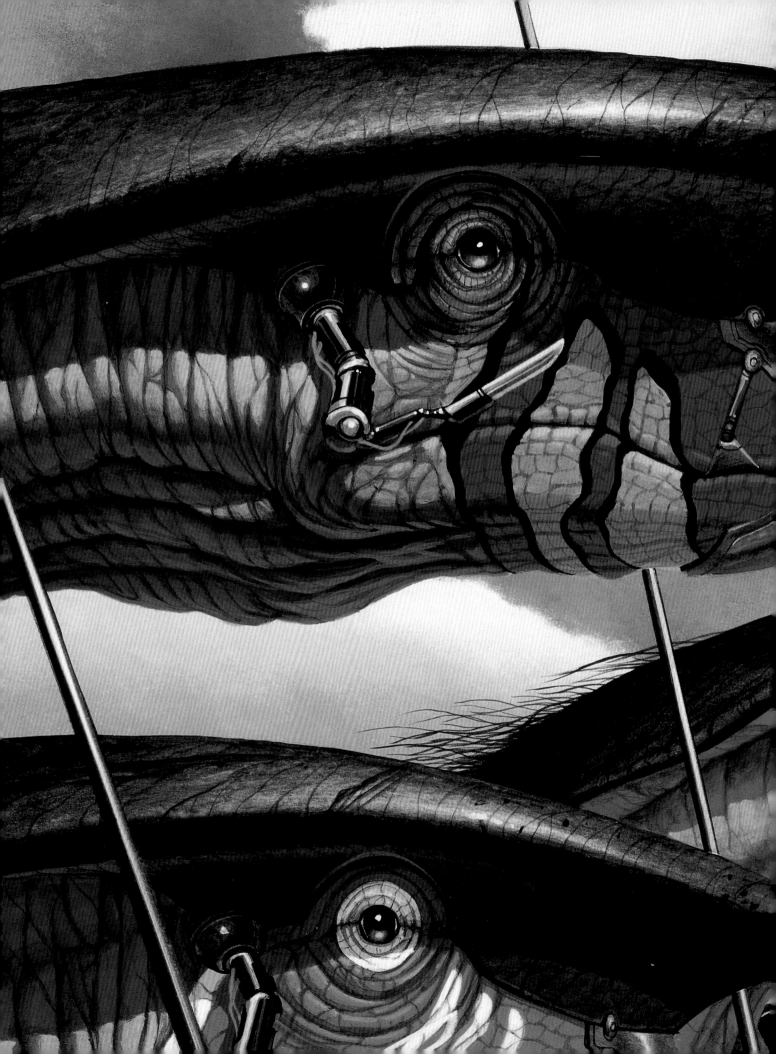

ease of ancient friendship. "You're back," they said. "Where were you? Why has all this death been done in your name?"

"Turn away from the slaughter," said Font Prime. Said Caps, "Come home to see me walk among you once again."

"He's a fraud!" cried Kaantur-Set. "The real Font Prime is dead! He died today!"

In reply, Caps remembered the scene with all the clarity of his mind — how it felt to be plucked into the air, caught by the feet, swung like a bludgeon against the cylinder. The memory of the shards spraying around him, the viscous fluid flowing, and that helpless body dangling from its life support.

Then, Kaantur's hands tearing the machinery from the ruined man. Kaantur's arm striking the ribs, smashing the heart, bringing the life that lingered there to a shuddering halt.

"Yet I am not dead," said Caps. "I transported myself out of the prison Kaantur made for me. I made myself anew, returned my memories into my mind, and I speak to you now more clearly than I ever could before. Come home and see me, my friends."

"Go forth and slay the last of the biological life!" cried Kaantur-Set. "Then come back and help me deal with this impostor, wherever he's hiding! You know that I am the strong one. You know that life belongs to the one who has in him the power to survive."

There were some who listened to Kaantur, and wanted to go on.

But in airboat after airboat, his followers shouted orders that the other robots would not obey. On land, the marching army turned back, leaving only a few still bent on destruction.

Too few. Despite their armaments, the followers of Kaantur-Set could easily see that they would be overwhelmed by the jodphurs and the humans fighting to defend their lives and homes, their children, their species.

Kaantur recognized it, too. The invasion would fail. He would expend the lives of his few supporters for nothing.

He also recognized something else. That while his numbers were few, the robots who followed him were the ones with the thirst for power, the ones unafraid to kill without qualm, his own kind.

All he had to do was find Caps and kill him, and the world would still belong to him. There would be plenty of time to cleanse Robota of biological life, when Font Prime was finally, fully dead.

So his followers turned back, too, and mingled with the returning armies. On the tree-killer airboats, they pretended to change, and thanked the crews that had resisted them. Many robots were fooled.

But Caps was not fooled. The invasion of the jodphur city had been stopped, but the war was not over yet, and soon Font Prime's enemies would be gathered in the city that floated in the air above this place.

Caps pulled himself away from the obsidian, but now he could feel the way it still clung to the memory of every cell of his skin. He was connected to the buried memory hidden in the skin of the world, skin to skin, and he could call upon it now without having to touch it, as Font Prime had called upon it and added to it from his prison in the cylinder that floated directly above this place.

Caps turned to look at the Servants who surrounded him. "Take me home," he said.

They returned to the airboat and it rose upward, reaching its docking station at the base of the dangling stone before any of the other airships could return. As it rose, as it docked, Caps spoke to Decan-Trap.

"I remember everything," he said. "I remember the messages I received every time I awoke. I know what they meant. I know who I am." Decan almost spoke then, but Caps held up a hand to stop him. "I know whom to kill," he said.

"I hoped you would," said Decan. "Because you had forgotten more than I knew."

9.5 The Hunter and the Hunted

"I remember even the things I didn't know I knew," said Caps. "Even the things my original, my fatherself, could not bring himself to face."

"The worst had already happened to him," said Decan. "And yet there were still things he dreaded."

"I once loved a woman," said Caps, "a wise and powerful woman, who stood at my side and loved me in return. We dreamed of what we could make of this world, with our robot friends, with the gifts of the Olm that had been bequeathed to us, some of which we had only just begun to understand."

"The woman you loved," said Decan softly.

"I was the teacher of the robots, and she the governor of the humans. But she resented the coming of her death, and was tempted by the power that we had only just discovered — to bond a living human mind to a robot, to become the robot. As I have linked my mind to the great memory deposits of the metals and crystals of Robota's crust, she linked her mind to a robot and rode it out boldly into the world even as her body was preserved in a cylinder of fluid."

"The name of the woman?" prompted Decan.

"Ansalilia," whispered Caps. "But what strode out of her chamber that day was nothing like the woman that I loved and trusted. She was a robot now, clinging to humanity only by such trivial means as smoking a pipe and playing the piano. She even denied her womanhood, calling herself Kaantur-Set."

"Do you still love her?" asked Decan-Trap. "Even now, will your love for her stay your hand?"

"Ansalilia is in my memory. Her body is in another cylinder, older than the one my original lived in. But the robot Kaantur-Set is not the woman I loved. Kaantur-Set is the murderer of my people."

The door opened. Two of Kaantur's hunter robots stood outside and fired their weapons point-blank at Caps's chest.

Ignoring the bloody wounds as if they were mosquito bites, Caps approached them, seized them by the throats, and dragged them down onto the floor. A Servant knelt over each one, reached into the cavity of its back, pressed the codes, and switched him off.

Then the Servant once again sprayed the wounds from which Caps bled profusely. The bleeding stopped. The wound was taped over. Caps went on.

< 9.6 A Flash of Memory

THE GHOST IN THE MACHINE

X

Beryl followed the sounds of the frantic piano, played by inhumanly fast fingers dancing over the keys. Beside her, a little behind, walked Elyseo. "What can you hope to do like this?" said Elyseo. "Alone like this, against Kaantur-Set?"

"I don't care what happens to me," said Beryl. "That makes me dangerous."

"Only to yourself," said Elyseo.

"That will be a nice change, to have the power to betray no one but myself."

"Beryl," said Elyseo, "can't you hear it? The voice of Font Prime, calling home the armies. Can't you hear?"

"I'm a human," said Beryl. "Human and nothing else. Bones of calcium, driven by muscle alone. Why should I be alive, when so many better souls are dead?"

"Because they're dead, and you're alive, and there's no benefit to them if you add yourself to their number."

Beryl ignored him and continued trying to find her way among the corridors to where the piano was being played.

In a vast chamber, a museum scattered with a thousand artifacts, Kaantur sat at a piano and played. But Kaantur-Set was not alone. A monkey paced the room, touching everything, the walls, the pillars, the hulks of inactive

> **10.1** Music of the Past

robots that slumped here and there. Little robots, huge ones, designs that Rend had seen nowhere else.

"Why all these toys?" asked Rend.

Kaantur-Set ignored him, went on playing.

Rend touched the knee of a giant robot that sat like a rag doll against a wall. "What are you for? New design, yet none of the new-built robots has a mind. So are you a mere machine, like the Guardians?"

There was no answer.

Into the museum strode Beryl, Elyseo just behind her.

"Kaantur!" she cried. "Come and show me how you can fight!"

The piano music hesitated only for a moment.

The slumping robot next to Rend suddenly shuddered. Rend leapt back. But the huge machine returned to dormancy, and Rend scampered away to see what Beryl was going to do.

"Give me my sister!" cried Beryl. "I paid the price, now give her to me!"

Over the sound of the piano, Kaantur said, "You didn't pay it, Beryl, darling. Juomes did."

"Where is she!"

"Where you'll never find her till I want you to," said Kaantur.

"Fight me!" cried Beryl.

"I don't intend to kill you," said Kaantur. "In fact, my plan is to let you and your precious sister live on after all the other biological life on earth is dead. I'll keep one garden so I can feed you, and then I can have the pleasure of watching you age and wither up and die, while I go on living, I and my kind."

"You have no *kind*," said Beryl. "Robots are dying out as well."

"Yes, they are, aren't they, the dear little toys."

That stopped Beryl only a couple of meters away from Kaantur's piano. "Toys? They're no more toys than you are."

"Toys," said Kaantur. "I'm tired of them. That's why I decided to put them all away."

"What are you talking about?" said Beryl.

"They were still useful to me in destroying all the life of Robota," said Kaantur. "Until Font Prime found his voice again. Now I'm tired of them. Their usefulness is over. I'll outlive them, too, the way I'll outlive human life."

10.2 Another Time, Another Place

"How do you think you'll kill all the robots?" asked Beryl.

"As easily as I stopped new ones from being built."

Elyseo circled behind Kaantur. "*You* stopped the making of new robots?"

"Who else but me and Font Prime understood what the Olm had done? Trickery and fraud. Thinking machines! What a laugh! No machine has ever had a thought in all the history of Robota. There has never been a sentient robot."

"I'm one," said Elyseo.

"No, my dear Servant, you only *think* you are."

"I think!" said Elyseo.

"Oh, of course. But the part of you that's robot doesn't think, and the part of you that thinks is not a robot." Kaantur suddenly left off playing, whirled around on the piano stool, and faced Elyseo. "What do you think those antibacterial treatments were all about?"

"Keeping us safe," said Elyseo. "From metal-eating bacteria the humans were trying to make."

"Oh, I'm sure it would work, too. But the real purpose was much more simple and direct. Once you all were thoroughly coated, no little organisms could creep out of your little metal noggins and infect the newly made robots. Therefore those organisms could not colonize the robotic brain and bring the thing to life. Therefore the robots remained dead machines, able to be trained, but never to learn, never to live."

"Organisms?" said Elyseo.

"You aren't a robot," said Kaantur. "You're a child of the Olm."

"The Olm are gone."

"The Olm who still walked in their ancient biological bodies are gone. We saw them fly away, you and I, Elyseo. But they left a colony of their children in this world, inhabiting the minds of the metal tools they taught us humans how to make."

"Us humans?" asked Beryl. "You think you're human? You really are insane."

"Font Prime and I discovered it," said Kaantur-Set. "Or, to be truthful, Font Prime discovered it. The Olm had found a way to make biological life interface so perfectly with electronic life that the Olm could create children who used robots as their bodies. Your robot brains are infested with the essence of the Olm. They live inside you like a disease. Except that the part of you that is truly you *is* the disease. The Olm infest you like bugs."

"I'm biological," said Elyseo.

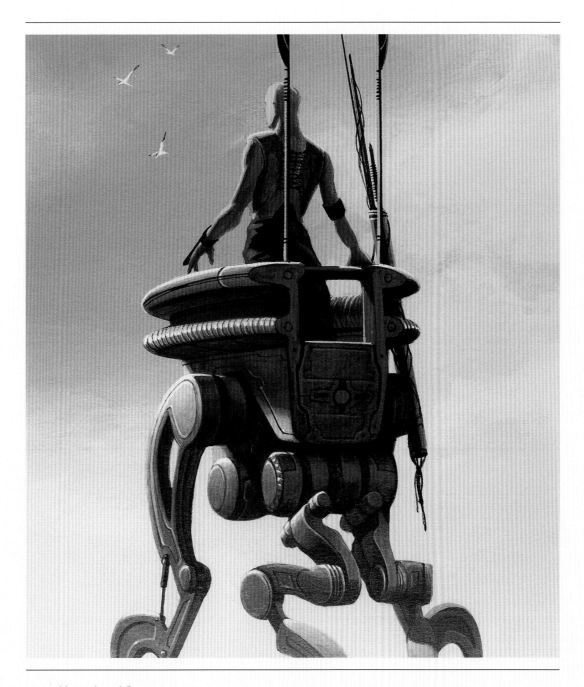

10.3 Memories of Caps

"And you're a human," said Beryl to Kaantur.

"Better than human," said Kaantur. "The next step. Font Prime did it first, connecting himself to interfaces that allowed him to use the very crust of the planet as his memory. It gave him the mental power to be able to run the teleporters, to see everything that happened in the world through every sense the biosphere could offer him. He played at being God.

"My aims," Kaantur went on, "were more modest. All I wanted was not to die. But my beloved Font Prime did not approve. He intended to live his natural life and pass away, to be replaced as the eyes and ears of the world by a child of ours — he thought. Only — and here's the real irony — I couldn't have children. My body of flesh had failed me. 'I love you anyway,' he told me. 'It's all right,' he told me.

"But it wasn't all right. It was the end of everything. It was death. His memory would be there in the planet's crust for his successor to pick up and keep alive, but when I died there'd be nothing at all, not even a child to carry on one feeble half of my genetic code."

Elyseo came closer. "Font Prime wouldn't let you bind yourself into a robot body."

"No, he said that it would be wrong, that robot bodies were for the children of the Olm, and humans had to be content with human bodies. How could that be right, for us to live

> 10.4 Kaantur's Proposition

our little century and disappear, while robots went on and on and on?"

"So you arranged a conspiracy to assassinate Font Prime," said Elyseo. "You plotted to kill your husband."

"Not kill him," said Kaantur. "Never that. If I had wanted him dead, he would have died back then. No, I wanted him to live, but with no choice but to link himself with a robot body as I wanted to. Only he wouldn't do it. Or he *said* he wouldn't do it. Secretly he was making that monster hybrid Caps, but all the time he pretended that he would never join me. So I let him rot! I let him dangle there in that sickening soup while *I* had my eternal life!

"And since he loved all that precious biological life, I'd put an end to it! I hunted them down, knowing that he could feel each death as if it happened in his own heart. He'd have to come out of the cylinder, wouldn't he? He'd have to come out and ride the machine the way I did!"

Kaantur turned to Beryl, picked up a picture from the top of the piano, and showed it to her. "Wasn't I a pretty thing?" she said. "Pretty as your sister. Prettier than you. He loved me then."

"But not now!" cried Caps from the museum door. "The woman I loved was not a murderer. The woman I loved was dead the moment she forced her memory into a cloned brain inside that robot shell."

Kaantur rose and walked toward Caps, ignoring the Servants gathered around. "My soldiers will be back soon. Enjoy yourself while you can. You're going to die. *These* won't defend you."

"I don't want them to," said Caps. "I don't need them to."

"Because we aren't going to fight anymore," said Kaantur-Set, "that's why. Because now that you're also riding the machine, you're going to stand beside me again, my husband again. We'll rule this world together. I'll even let your little biosphere go on living, since it amuses you. You can have your jodphurs, your hunter-beasts, your talking monkeys. I'll even stop having the robots treated with this spray."

Kaantur-Set touched an antibacterial unit that was exhibited on a table. "You can make as many more as you want. All you have to do is love me again."

"Love what?" said Caps. "There's no Ansalilia now. Only a murderous machine infected with a disease."

"Ansalilia is still alive, you fool," said Kaantur-Set. She strode to one of the pillars, stroked it . . . and a panel rose up, revealing inside it a wrinkled woman's body on life support inside a cylinder like the one that had once held Font Prime. "There I am, the love of your life, the beautiful Ansalilia." She whirled on Caps. "That's what you wanted me to become! Old, hideous, a monster, and then I'd die with that wrinkled body the only thing I had to show for my few years of life! *That* is what you wanted to make of me!"

Caps turned to Elyseo. "She hasn't mastered the technique of it after all," he said. "She has to have her original body living. She couldn't transfer herself completely into the robot, the way the Olm did, the way my original did."

Elyseo laughed. "And she thinks she's superior to us? She's the weakest of us all."

Kaantur roared in fury and threw herself on Elyseo, who made no move to defend himself. Kaantur would have torn his head off, but Caps sprang across the room in two huge steps and pulled her away. He threw her against the cylinder where her human body floated, and cracks spread out along the surface from the point of impact. Just what Kaantur had done to Font Prime's cylinder.

"You can't do that!" screamed Kaantur-Set. "You love me! You promised you'd love me forever!"

"Let's see," said Caps. "When you had assassins blow me up, when you confined me inside that cylinder for generations, I think my promise of undying love for you ended."

Kaantur-Set screamed and flung herself upon Caps. At once Beryl grabbed a battle staff and joined in the fight, even though she couldn't

match either of them for strength. She went for the coded place in Kaantur's back. And with Caps distracting Kaantur, fighting her, pulling her this way and that, Beryl was able to reach in, press the code . . .

Kaantur-Set went still and slumped down into a sitting posture on the floor.

"And that's that," said Beryl.

With a roar, the largest of the robots lurched into life. "Do you think I only implanted myself into *one* machine?" cried Kaantur-Set, her voice now the harsh metallic roar of the monster. "I told you I didn't need you weaker creatures! I can have as many bodies as I like! I'm an entire species by myself. Kaantur-Set, shape-changer! Kaantur-Set, mother of all children, and every single one of them is *meeeee.*"

The huge new Kaantur reached out, picked Beryl up from the ground, poked a giant finger through her belly, and flung her bleeding body against a wall. She fell limply to the ground and did not move.

"Beryl!" cried Caps. "No!"

"You thought you could abandon me for some girl," said Kaantur. "I knew it would happen. As I got older, you'd think that you, the powerful man, the god of Robota, you deserved a *young* bride, not the old crone who couldn't even have babies."

10.5 The Fight

"The old crone I would have loved," said Font Prime. "I would have been faithful to you."

"And we both would have been dead three hundred years ago! Face it, Caps, old fellow, I saved both our lives!"

"Until you ended mine."

"You're still alive."

"No thanks to you," said Caps.

Then he dashed for the cylinder that held Kaantur's body and smashed a fist against the surface. It sprang leaks, just as Font Prime's cylinder had done. But it did not break.

Before Caps could strike again, the giant Kaantur robot was on him, picking him up and tossing him around like a doll.

"How does it feel, my love, my darling!" screamed Kaantur-Set. "How does it feel to be a doll for somebody else to control!"

Decan and the other Servants were watching now, impassive. Elyseo turned to them. "Aren't you going to do something?"

"We are doing something," said Decan-Trap. "We're watching a lovers' quarrel."

"He's going to die! We're supposed to watch over Font Prime, and he's going to —"

"If you'd stop shouting and listen, you'd hear what Font Prime is asking us to do." Decan took off at a run for the spot where Beryl's limp body lay against a wall. At once he and a couple of Servants were working on her, putting her back together while the fight went on.

If it could be called a fight. Kaantur threw Caps, then chased him down and threw him again almost before he could pick himself up. One of Caps's arms was hanging useless, and it was only a matter of moments before Kaantur succeeded in breaking him into pieces.

Elyseo picked up the antibacterial apparatus from the exhibit table, then strode to Rend, put the monkey on the apparatus and the hose in the monkey's hand, then hoisted it all onto his shoulders. When Kaantur passed near them on the way to pick up Caps's flung body once again, Elyseo leapt up onto the monster's back.

"Wasting your time!" cried Kaantur with a laugh. "I had this one built without deactivation codes."

They weren't going for the codes. Elyseo sat on Kaantur's shoulders, straddling her giant neck, and pressed several releases in order to open up her head. "Now!" he cried, and Rend began squirting antibacterial spray into the wide-open metal cranium.

The giant robot body danced around insanely, while Kaantur's voice moaned. "What did you do? What's happening?"

Then the giant robot's arm swung against the cylinder and broke it open. Fluid gushed out. The aging body of the woman Ansalilia toppled out onto the floor.

Her feeble hand reached up and pried the life-support mask from her own face. While the giant robot slumped inertly, the ancient woman crept across the floor, reaching out to Caps, speaking in a husky whisper. "You said you'd love me . . . forever. You said I would always be . . . beautiful . . ."

And then she coughed, gagged, choked, died.

Caps walked to her. Knelt beside her. Cradled the ghastly old head in his lap with his one good arm. Two Servants knelt beside him and started working on his injuries, opening the skin to repair damage to his robot arms and back.

"Ansalilia," murmured Caps. "You could have been a legend, a beautiful memory. Now you're a tale to frighten children. The monster in the night. The beast who tore at the heart of the world."

He laid her down again upon the ground and walked, still uncertain of his steps, to where they worked on Beryl. "Is she alive?"

"Not conscious, but alive," said Decan-Trap.

"I know where her sister is. Now that Kaantur-Set is dead, her secrets are all laid bare before me. If Beryl's going to die, she first should see her sister alive and free."

Two Servants rushed from the museum to get the girl.

"And now we wait," said Elyseo, "because there's nothing we can do."

"I'm a monkey," said Rend. "I can always do something."

Rend sat on the back of the piano, his feet dangling over the keyboard, and began playing a tune with his toes. Elyseo sat down before him and, reaching to left and right, played an accompaniment. Caps listened to it as the Servants worked expertly to try to repair the damage to Beryl's body. If she died, he thought, she would die with music in her ears. But perhaps the tune would calm her, call her back, remind her of the music of life, dissonance resolving into harmony if you could only hold on long enough.

>> 10.6 Ansalilia

XI

BROTHERS AND SISTERS

11.1 The Lion and the Lamb

In a forest clearing, Caps set a stone marker in place at the head of a large grave. The resting place of Juomes. A few meters away, there was another grave, human size. A young girl, perhaps fourteen years old, touched the stone. "She was the only parent I remember," said the girl. "Father and mother both. I know she did awful things. I know she tried to kill you. All of that." She lifted a tear-streaked face. "But she's stopped doing bad things now. So it's all right that I remember loving her, isn't it?"

Beryl embraced her sister.

Decan, Elyseo, and several humans, jodphurs, hunter-beasts, and a monkey named Rend all stood around Juomes's grave, each walking up in turn to touch the stone.

Caps — Font Prime — walked away to join the girls at Ansalilia's grave. "There's nothing wrong with missing someone that you love. I do, even though I lost her long before her body died, and never had a chance to mourn."

Slowly, and after some hesitation, Beryl's arm reached out to take Caps around the waist. They stood like that at the graveside for a long while. Then, with Beryl holding her sister by one hand and Caps by the other, they walked back among the children of humanity and the children of the Olm.

The people of Robota.

> **11.2** Caps and Rend

ACKNOWLEDGMENTS

My deepest appreciation to all my friends who have generously supported and assisted me in realizing this dream. Special thanks to David Craig, Kathryn Otoshi, Tony McVey, Warren Fu, John Duncan, Kim Smith, Mike Murnane, John Goodson, Giles Hancock, Pam Statz, and Marc Hedlund.

And finally, thanks to my mom, dad, brother, and sister.

— Doug Chiang

Photograph by Giles Hancock

DOUG CHIANG has worked in film and television production since 1986, earning an Academy Award, two British Academy Awards, and a Clio. For 13 years, he has worked for Lucasfilm Ltd., serving as creative director from 1993–1995 for Industrial Light and Magic, a division of Lucas Digital. In 1995, he became design director for the *Star Wars* prequels, *Episode I* and *II*. His paintings are exhibited nationally in a variety of forms, including book covers and limited edition prints. He lives in Northern California with his wife and two children.

Photograph by Bob Henderson

ORSON SCOTT CARD is a preeminent sci-fi author with more than 100 titles to his credit, including the beloved classic *Ender's Game* and the national bestseller *Ender's Shadow*, for which he won the Hugo and Nebula awards. In addition to science fiction, Card has written several plays and two books on the craft of writing and his works have been translated into many languages, including Catalan, Danish, Dutch, Finnish, French, German, Hebrew, Italian, Japanese, Polish, Portuguese, Romanian, Russian, Slovakian, Spanish, and Swedish. He and his wife live in Greensboro, North Carolina, and are the parents of five children.